THE QUANTUM JULY

THE QUANTUM JULY

Ron King

Delacorte Press

Published by Delacorte Press
an imprint of Random House Children's Books
a division of Random House, Inc.
New York

Delacorte Press and colophon are registered trademarks of
Random House, Inc.

www.randomhouse.com/teens

Educators and librarians, for a variety of teaching tools, visit us at
www.randomhouse.com/teachers

Library of Congress Cataloging-in-Publication Data
King, Ron.
The quantum July / by Ron King. — 1st ed.
p. cm.
Summary: As problems escalate between their parents, a Harvard-educated stock boy and
a would-be physicist, thirteen-year-old Danny agrees to participate in his twelve-year-old
sister's experiments with quantum physics, through which he hopes he can change their
lives for the better.
ISBN 978-0-385-73418-9 (trade) — ISBN 978-0-385-90432-2 (lib. bdg.) [I. Quantum
theory—Fiction. 2. Space and time—Fiction. 3. Family problems—Fiction. 4. Brothers and
sisters—Fiction. 5. Self-actualization—Fiction.] I. Title.
PZ7.K58913Qua 2007
[Fic]—dc22
2007002409

The text of this book is set in 11-point Stones Informal.

Printed in the United States of America

10 9 8 7 6 5 4 3 2 1

First Edition

To Suzanne, the best choice I ever made

If quantum mechanics hasn't profoundly shocked you, you haven't understood it yet.

Niels Bohr, physicist (1885–1962)

. . . And science is nothing but the finding of analogy, identity, in the most remote parts.

Ralph Waldo Emerson
from *The American Scholar*

1

If Danny Parsons had known he was about to "unleash the power of the quantum world"—which was how his little sister, Bridget, referred to it—or if he'd had even the slightest clue that in two hours the shed he was leaning against was going to explode in a fireball of near–Big Bang proportions, he probably would have had an easier time staying awake. As it was, he sat in the shade, let his eyes slowly close, and tried to keep from drooling on himself.

Part of the problem was that it was July and hot. And the other part of the problem was that, on the other side of the wall he was leaning against, his mother was scribbling physics equations on a chalkboard. That reminded him of Mrs. Ferguson's seventh-grade math class. And that made him droopy. His eyes drooped until they were shut, and his chin sagged and hung from his mouth, just about resting on his chest.

Math had always had that effect on him. It was in Mrs.

Ferguson's math class that he'd broken his personal record for most consecutive days of falling asleep in school. Seventy-two. That added up to almost half a year. It might even have been a record for the entire seventh grade. His brother, Simon, who had just turned sixteen, liked to brag that when he was in seventh grade, he fell asleep seventy-seven times, but that was in Mrs. Ruskin's English class, where she was always playing Beethoven and Bach in the background, which was completely unfair. Plus, it was right after lunch, which was also completely unfair. Who *wouldn't* fall asleep? No, in Danny's mind, seventy-two third-period math naps with Mrs. Ferguson was a far bigger accomplishment. Especially considering that during the entire class she would constantly lean over Danny's shoulder and shout, "Wrong, wrong, wrong," in his ear. He would have liked to see Simon fall asleep under those conditions.

"Danny, wake up!"

"The answer is seventy-two," Danny said, his eyes startled and wide. He sat up and searched for the blackboard, the math problems, and tried to shield himself from the scorn of Mrs. Ferguson. But she wasn't there. Instead he saw the yard, his house, the barn just off to his left. He breathed a bit more easily and leaned his head against the shed. He could hear his mother on the other side of the wall. It was summer. He wasn't in school after all.

Bridget, his twelve-year-old sister, glared at him. "Will you quiet down? Do you want her to hear us?"

"Well, stop scaring me," he said. He wiped the sweat from his forehead and shook out an arm that had started to fall asleep. "Anything happening yet?"

2

"Not yet," Bridget said.

His eyes drooped again.

Danny didn't mean to abandon his sister in the middle of their spying activities, but dreaming, dropping off for a moment no matter where he was, was one of the best things in his life. He dreamed—sometimes fully asleep, and sometimes by slipping into that strange place that lies between sleep and wakefulness—all the time, one minute aware of the world around him and then, in a second, drifting into a dream about a different life in another time, a dream about the life he might have lived if he hadn't been kidnapped.

The dreams weren't about *being* kidnapped. They were dreams about a world that had somehow gone wrong—put him in the wrong family, the wrong place. They were dreams that tried to help Danny make sense of his life, because as far as he was concerned, one thing was certain: he wasn't supposed to be Danny Parsons at all. In his heart, in his very soul, he was supposed to be somebody else, somebody important. And his dreams helped him discover who that might be.

He'd been creating these dreams and making up stories about himself for years, but for the past year, thanks to subscriptions to *National Geographic* and *Smithsonian* magazines, his stories had been getting much better. He used photos from the magazines to make the sights—and even the sounds and smells—so real and lifelike that he'd suddenly find that he'd been lost in a dream for hours at a time. He dreamed in bed, at the dinner table, and most often at school. That was his primary activity for about half of his time in seventh grade, though Mrs. Ferguson and his other teachers hadn't seemed to notice.

But his classmates had. Danny's reputation as a perpetual dreamer was well established. He was the kid who was always "out to lunch," "zoned out." "Danny Parsons," kids said, "lights on but nobody's home." There wasn't a kid at school who didn't know him as the space cadet.

Including Sarah Evans.

But a part of him almost didn't care, because the fact was that the stories were so much better than his actual life, so much more exciting and *real*.

In his imagined life he could become the second son of an Arab sultan. He could walk down a Cairo street and smell the camels, feel the dust and heat and noise of Egyptian life. Or he could be the second son of a Scandinavian reindeer breeder and, just as Mrs. Ferguson was explaining how to solve for x, he'd find himself wincing at the cold, squinting in the blinding light of the Arctic sun. He'd gotten pretty good at it. The dream stories were perfect.

And there were moments when, in his own mind, he ceased being Danny Parsons, the second son of Wade Parsons, the Harvard-educated stock boy. He became, instead, the second son of a great and powerful man, standing before the wonders of the world in a seersucker suit, the smells of exotic spices and ancient dust surrounding him until he felt himself standing taller, breathing easier, with confidence, so that he felt that if he held his hand out to a dark-haired, blue-eyed girl, she'd be glad to take it.

This time, as he sat outside the shed in his backyard,

his chin sank slowly to his chest and he began to dream that he was the second son of an international undercover agent who had brought him to a laboratory on the outskirts of Prague to spy on a top-secret nuclear physicist.

The Czechoslovakian sun is hotter than usual and, in spite of the tension surrounding the spying and the intrigue and the cool way his father's German-made pistol makes his pocket bulge, Danny finds himself repeatedly distracted by a group of young people his age who take the benches beside them. One of the girls has dark hair and blue eyes and she reminds him of someone, if he could only think who it is, but his father places his hand firmly in the middle of Danny's back and leads him silently into the shade, where they wait for the moment when the secrets of the universe will be revealed to them. Just Danny and his father. Together. And in the dream Danny knows that this is what he has been waiting for his entire life, although, for some reason, every now and again he steals a look over his shoulder at the girl on the bench behind him.

Bridget grabbed his arm. "Shhh!" she said, even though he hadn't said a word. "Listen."

Danny blinked in the light that reflected off the roof of the barn and rubbed his arm, which had fallen asleep for real this time. Behind him, the tapping and scratching on the blackboard had been growing increasingly intense. It was as if his mother were trying to beat the truth out of the formulas she was writing.

All of a sudden, it went silent inside the shed. There

was a pause of a few seconds, and then they heard her footsteps across the floor.

Bridget jumped to her feet and ran to the corner of the shed just as her mother stepped through the door. Danny followed her, shaking his arm back to life.

Claire Parsons stood in the sun and lifted her face to the sky. Her skin was clear and pink, her eyes dark and hardened. She was beautiful in many ways, but there was an incongruity to her features that made her face seem slightly out of balance. Her nose was just a bit too big, her chin a bit too pointed, her cheeks a bit too . . . something, so that Danny could never decide if she was beautiful or not.

But at that moment she looked radiant. Her hair was standing up in the front, as though she'd had her hand on her forehead for a long time. Her face was flushed and she looked a little lost and entirely glad about it. Her pants were covered with chalk, the hair at her temples was wet from perspiration, and she had a faraway smile on her face. She looked powerful and smart, and, to Danny, a little crazy. She reminded him of the classic mad scientist; her hair had curled in the humidity and her cheeks glowed under the dusting of chalk. She practically floated as she wandered away from the shed and across the lawn toward the house.

She was the kind of woman a man follows, Danny thought, and he started to walk in her direction.

But Bridget grabbed him by the shirt. "What are you doing? Come on," she said, and she yanked him so hard that he almost lost his balance. When he turned around, she had already darted around the corner and squeezed through the half-open door of the shed.

Danny followed. He felt as if he was always following Bridget, which sometimes bothered him. He *was* older, after all. A whole year older.

Not that that made much of a difference. He knew without really knowing that Bridget was exactly like their mother. She was the kind of girl a boy just follows. So he followed her into the shed. Into their mother's physics laboratory.

Into, as it turned out, the mysteries of the universe.

2

There were two places in the world that Danny loved more than any other. The first was the barn, which was old and dusty and smelled like the past—the past before the land had been sold to developers, when the barn had housed horses and tractors, when the farm had been alive, full of animals and fields of corn and the hum of life just under the surface of things. It smelled of animals and motor oil, dust and manure and silage.

But it also smelled like the past that *might* have been. When he was younger, Danny had spent hours in the upper loft, making up dreams about the life that he might have lived if, for example, he'd only been allowed to grow up in the Yukon instead of being shipped to New Hampshire. He'd lie in collapsed bales of hay and straw and the details of a life *almost* lived would float around him and settle in his mind like the pieces of dust and pollen floating in the streaks of light that poked through the barn walls.

His other favorite place—and for almost the opposite reason—was the shed.

For years it had been used to store old bikes and lawn equipment, but a few years ago his mother had turned it into a physics laboratory. She put a desk in a corner and covered the walls with chalkboards and bookshelves. She purchased a used oscilloscope and an electromagnetic generator from one of the state colleges and spent several years assembling one of the best personal science libraries in the area.

Over her desk she'd hung two framed diplomas, one for her undergraduate degree in physics and the other for her graduate degree in particle physics. Next to the diplomas was a framed letter that congratulated her on receiving the LeRoy Apker Award from the American Physical Society, a national award given to only two undergraduate students each year. The award was so impressive that it earned her a graduate fellowship at M.I.T.—a fellowship she had turned down when her first child, Simon, was born.

Danny found it all completely fascinating. If the barn was about a lost past, the shed was about an imagined future. It was about the *possibility* of things to come. In the shed, it didn't matter that Danny lived the most boring life he could imagine, because standing among the shelves of equipment and books an entire future unfolded before him. In the shed, he could become a great scientist. He could go on to cure diseases, uncover the mysteries of strange and disgusting habits of insects, discover the secret of his brother Simon's repulsive eating habits. For his mother, he could find a cure for belching and flatulence.

He remembered the experiment his mother had performed last summer with equipment she'd borrowed from the high school. All morning she'd kept herself locked in the shed, and then, when they were on the porch eating lunch, this enormous bolt of electricity jumped from the shed, struck the antenna at the top of the house and blew up their television. It was amazing. Remembering that moment, Danny thought if science could do that, what couldn't it do? He looked around the shed. Everything in that space held the key to some perfect understanding of the world. He was so close to it, it was as if he could almost *touch* it.

The problem was that Danny didn't actually *get* science.

But Bridget understood science completely.

She went straight to the board.

There were three blackboard panels lining the walls of the shed, every one of them covered with their mother's writing. Danny assumed that the formulas had to do with math, but now he wasn't quite sure. For one thing, there was hardly a single number on the entire board. Everything was a letter or a symbol like λ or θ or Σ, and they were all gathered in these strange groups. Danny recognized some of the symbols from algebra, and it made him sleepy just looking at it.

"What is it?" he asked.

"I don't know."

"I thought you were a genius."

She glared at him. "Having an IQ of a hundred and fifty-three doesn't mean that you're born with all the answers, brainless."

Danny just smiled. "Oh," he said. Then he waited a few seconds. "Figure it out yet?"

Bridget rolled her eyes. "Why don't you go drag your knuckles to the other side of the room."

"This is more fun."

She ignored him, something she'd recently learned to do. Where did girls learn these things? he wondered. Simon said girls had a gene that switched on when they turned twelve and made every girl in the world a "master of cool disdain." If that was true, Bridget's had definitely been triggered. She ignored him like a real pro—something she'd been doing a lot lately. Which was probably why it felt strangely familiar to him.

For about a minute he watched her concentrate on the formula. She was nodding and mumbling to herself, her brows drawn together and her hand readjusting her glasses as they slid down her nose on beads of sweat. But watching Bridget try to figure out a physics formula was about as exciting as watching Mrs. Ferguson factor a quadratic equation for the 756th time.

He turned from the board and walked among the mysteries of science, his mind wandering into the possibilities of the lives he could live as his hands randomly touched the objects that filled the shed almost to overflowing.

Of all the places his mother loved, the shed was, in many ways, the most unlike her. Everything in her life was about order and control: how she dressed, the way she organized the house, the bookshelves, the laundry. It all fit a pattern, made sense.

But the shed was different. It was a total mess. Ramps and ball bearings lay in heaps beside pendulums and springs. Spools of wire were piled beside a half-full plastic tray of water and a car battery. Protractors, magnifying glasses, and a few small electric engines littered several shelves of a bookcase that was wedged in between some old yard tools, a broken lawn mower, a plastic gallon container of gasoline, and several quarts of motor oil. A stopwatch hung across the eyepiece of a large telescope that stood near the window.

It was a dusty place, but it was full of light, and their mother had hung dozens of prisms around the room that slowly spun and splashed tiny rainbows of light across the walls. "The artists of physics," she called them. And crammed in a small cluttered corner beside the old Schwinn three-speed sat her desk.

There wasn't a clean space on the entire surface. Papers, pencils, and books—some lying open, others stacked flat in piles—covered every inch of the desk. Her lamp cast a halo of light on the center, where dust particles moved in circular patterns or fell slowly into the gathering film that covered the work space.

It reminded him of Bridget's room. It was all confusion and disorder, and it all somehow made sense to their mother. And maybe, he thought, that's why it made sense to Bridget, too.

"Don't touch anything," Bridget cautioned without taking her eyes from the board in front of her.

"Why not?"

"Because you make me nervous."

"I make you nervous?"

"Ever since Grampa Joe got sick."

"Because I cried? I make you nervous because I cried? It happened to be a very sad thing."

"It isn't just that," she said, turning to him and staring over her glasses, which had slid once more down her nose, "but yes. You cried before you had a reason to cry. Like you just *knew*."

"So?"

"And remember what you were holding?"

"Coincidence."

"Maybe," she said. "But I'm not taking any chances. The data all points to the same conclusion."

"What data?"

She numbered the items off on her fingers. "You were holding a photo of Grampa Joe, Dad called a family meeting, you started crying like you already knew what he'd say, and it was like the photo told you, like holding it gave you some weird insight. I can't explain it, but I saw how you stared at that picture and how your fingers moved like they were tingling. The whole thing is weird and you know it is."

"That happened six months ago."

"Exactly. Only six months ago you did something very weird."

"Knock it off, B. Six months is forever. And besides, it was *nothing*."

"You can say what you like. All I know is that what happened with you and Grampa Joe's death doesn't make any logical sense, and that kind of thing makes me nervous. So, just to be safe, keep your hands to yourself." She turned back to the board. "I mean it," she said. "Don't touch *anything*."

Bossed around by a twelve-year-old again. He would have protested, but in a way he knew Bridget was right. When Grampa Joe had gotten sick, Danny had known before anyone even suspected. But he didn't know in the way Bridget thought he knew. It wasn't a vision or "insight" or anything like that at all. It was more as if he felt that one of the stories in his head had come true. It *felt* true.

He was having one of his dreams the afternoon his father called that last family meeting. He'd been imagining his life as the kidnapped son of a famous Catalan architect. But in his dream one person knew the truth about him. One person could explain him to himself, help him understand his unique place in the world. One person knew who he was supposed to be, and that person was Grampa Joe. And then, just before his father called the meeting, Danny's dream shifted and he could see himself standing beside the bed where Grampa Joe lay, cold and stiff, and in Grampa Joe's hands were a pen and a pad of paper on which he'd begun to record the truth about Danny's life. But he'd never finished. The truth had died with him.

And Danny *had* been holding a photograph of Grampa

Joe. It had been taken decades earlier, when Grampa Joe was visiting Danny's father, who was studying in Barcelona, Spain, for a year. He was standing in front of the great cathedral, la Sagrada Familia, and he looked so young and happy. He looked as if he was living a dream—as if he was living *Danny's* dream. Danny was staring at the photograph when his father called them all into the living room. And in that moment, Danny's real world and his dream world seemed to come together. And he just knew. Grampa Joe was about to die, and with him would die the truth about his real identity. Now no one would know that he really belonged in Barcelona, that his father was world-famous, that his life in the Parsons family was just a big mistake.

No one would know who he was supposed to be. *Danny* himself wouldn't know who he was supposed to be. And he felt utterly lost. Completely, utterly lost.

And *that* was why he cried.

But this wasn't exactly the kind of thing he could *tell* people, especially not Bridget. Her world was defined by theories and proofs, ideas and facts. Knowing that his grandfather was going to die wasn't a fact, really. It wasn't like he could *explain* it, and he definitely didn't want to try.

Except she was right about one thing: he had been holding that photograph, and that seemed to have made a difference.

"Fine," he conceded. "I won't touch anything, although I think you're being ridiculous."

"Thank you," Bridget said, her eyes again fixed on the board.

Danny wandered back over to his mother's desk, where a book had been left open. "Hey, this looks interesting."

Bridget came over and picked up the book, closing it quickly to read the cover. It was titled *Chaos Theories,* and it was written by David Evans. "Whoa," she said.

"What are chaos theories?"

"They're ways of explaining entropy."

"Entropy?"

She nodded. "It's how scientists measure the way the universe is always moving from order to disorder, like why things rust or break down or move from neat and tidy to messy and junky."

"Like your room?"

She looked at him without speaking. After staring at him for almost ten full seconds, she said, "Very funny."

Danny smiled. "So?" he said. "Is it like your room?"

She pushed her glasses up onto her nose and shrugged. "Sort of."

Something about the equations in the book looked familiar to Danny. "Now, I'm no genius, but it seems to me that this formula looks a lot like that one," he said, pointing to the board.

Bridget carried the book over to the second panel and followed the equation with her finger as she checked it against the book. "Whoa," she said again.

"What?"

"The equations are exactly the same until right here."

"What does that mean?"

"It looks like Mom's been making some improvements to Professor Evans's theories."

16

"Professor Evans from the college?"

She nodded.

"The same Professor Evans who is the father of Sarah Evans?"

Bridget smiled. "Yes." She studied him almost as carefully as she'd studied the chalkboards. "Why do you mention Sarah?"

"I don't know," he said. "She's in my class. She has the same name. I happen to *know* her. That's why."

"No other reason?" Bridget taunted.

"No."

"Just checking," she said.

Danny stood in front of the formula and let his mind wander. He thought about Sarah Evans and how she might look at him differently if he were standing before her in a long white coat, explaining to a team of lab assistants on the International Space Station the data he'd collected from a probe his research team had launched into the core of the sun. How might she feel about him if he were famous, if he were a hero? He imagined running into her at an awards ceremony, where he was signing his new book, which combined chaos theory and—he tried to think of another science theory, but all he could come up with was spontaneous combustion. Still, it sounded good. Sarah would be impressed. Spontaneous combustion, he was certain, would revolutionize the science world.

He imagined Sarah beside him as he reached his hand out and just brushed it against the board. His fingers, wet with perspiration, smudged the formula and left three streaks across the slate.

Bridget was on him in a second. She grabbed his arm and pulled it from the board. "I said don't touch *anything.*"

Danny yanked his hand away from her. "So I touched it," he said, his voice rising with indignation. "So what? It's a stupid math problem. It's not like it's the launch code for a SCUD missile."

Bridget just shook her head. "Come with me," she said, taking his arm. "Something weird is happening, just like with Grampa Joe. I feel it. I don't know what's going on with you, but I'm getting you out of here before you do some real damage." With a firm grip on his sleeve, she pulled him across the room to the door.

"You're weird."

She laughed sarcastically. "*I'm* weird?"

"They're just math problems. It's not like someone's life is at stake."

"That's what I would have thought about Grampa Joe's picture."

"Do you think I *caused* Grampa Joe's death?"

"Don't be ridiculous," she said. "Of course not. But you *knew* things, Danny. It was almost like you were able to be there with Grampa Joe and also with me. And that doesn't make any sense. And therefore, it makes me very nervous. Now, out!" She pushed him through the door into the sunlight.

"So that's it?" he said. "We're just going to leave?"

"No," she said. "I'm going to find out what Mom is up to."

"What are you going to do? Ask her?" he called after Bridget as she headed across the lawn.

She thought for a moment. "I don't know yet. But I want to know what she's doing. Besides," she said, glaring at him one more time, "something about you is making me very nervous, Danny Parsons."

Danny shrugged. "I'm a danger to others," he said, mocking her. "But you should know. You're the genius."

3

Lunch had already begun when they arrived. Simon was sitting at the counter reading *Baseball Digest* with his hand buried in a box of croutons. He could eat anything, any time of day, and his odd habits concerning food were consistent with his personality and appearance, both of which were also a little unorthodox. He was tall and handsome. His face was narrow, and that made his eyes and mouth appear bigger than they really were. But there was something striking about the arrangement of his features. As with his mother, a certain incongruity blended into something unique and surprising and nice to look at. His personality worked in this same way, a mixture of kindness and generosity that he punctuated with flashes of vicious sarcasm and outright meanness. He was funny in the cruelest ways, but he was also the most thoughtful child in the Parsons family.

He was going into eleventh grade and his plan was to work out at the batting cages for most of the summer and winter, with the hope of making the varsity baseball team. He had his sights set on a baseball scholarship to the college, if his grades and his batting average continued to improve.

Across from Simon, Claire Parsons stood eating a tuna sandwich. On her face, she still wore that same faraway, dreamy look she had had when she first left the shed. Danny noticed that she wasn't quite *glowing*, but there was still something in her smile that made him feel a little funny inside.

Danny and Bridget made peanut butter and jelly sandwiches. Danny poured milk and Bridget got napkins and an apple for them to split. They sat at the table. No one said a word. Danny could tell that Bridget was still puzzling over the meaning of those figures and equations. He tapped his fingers on the table as he chewed and thought about a song he had heard last year in history class, when they were studying world cultures—his favorite subject. It was an Irish tune that had stayed with him. He heard it in his mind, and then his thoughts wandered until he imagined a life where he was born in an Irish town on the coast to a father who was a world-renowned musician. Danny had learned to accompany him on the bodhran—that drum that you held with one hand as you strummed on the surface of it with the other. People came from as far away as Dublin to hear them.

At the table he beat a rhythm against his plate that got faster and faster. Then he started chewing to the beat. He could almost smell the mist off the Irish Sea as it soaked into his warm wool sweater.

"What are you singing, sweetie?"

Danny almost bit his tongue in surprise. "Nothing," he mumbled.

His mother smiled as she sat beside him at the table. "Don't talk with your mouth full, please."

Danny shot a glance at Simon, who sat just out of his mother's vision. His mouth was so full of croutons that his cheeks might have burst, but his jaw was motionless and he caught Danny's eye and smiled, opening his mouth wide and revealing a crunched crouton mash.

"Sorry," Danny said.

He took another bite of his sandwich and glanced sideways at his mother. *She looks more like herself,* he thought as he watched her flip through a pile of mail she'd brought from the counter. Her hair wasn't standing up in front anymore and she'd lost that glow in her eyes. She moved through the stack of mail with the same efficiency he was used to seeing. Almost everything about the shed— the confusion, the mystery, the mad-scientist *magic* (he couldn't think of another word to describe it)—had left her. She was herself again. Claire Parsons.

Danny watched her shuffle past some bills, a notice from the Free Tibet Society—his father was a charter member—and a seed catalog. She pulled out a letter. "Simon? Looks like you got a note."

He almost choked on a crouton. "Who's it from?" he mumbled, crumbs falling from his mouth.

"From the large, curly script on the envelope, I doubt it's a letter from a college scout."

He took the letter from her and furrowed his brow.

"I bet it's from Monica," Bridget said. She smiled at Danny.

"What is it?" Danny asked.

Simon ran a finger along the flap of the envelope and pulled out what looked like a page torn from a magazine. "It's nothing."

"It looks like a survey," Bridget said. "Did she send you a love survey? From *Seventeen* or something?"

"Maybe," he said, folding it and shoving it into his back pocket.

"Oh, don't put it away. Let's *take* it," she cried. "Then we can send it back to her."

"Forget it," Simon said.

"Please," Bridget begged. "What's the first question? 'Do you like chocolate better than flowers?' "

"I like chocolate better than flowers," Danny said.

"Too bad no one sends *you* a survey," Simon said.

Bridget smiled. "Sarah Evans is too classy to send a survey from *Seventeen*. She's not a bimbo like Monica."

"Shut up, Bridget," Danny and Simon said at the same time.

"That's enough," their mother said. "And Bridget, please do not use that word again. No one deserves to be called a bimbo. You wouldn't like it, and I'm sure Monica doesn't like it either."

"But Mom," Bridget said. "She *is* a bimbo. Isn't she, Simon?"

He shrugged. "Sort of, I guess."

"Be that as it may," their mother said, "we won't rub it in. Certainly not during lunch."

She riffled through the rest of the mail, making a stack of catalogs to recycle before she even looked through them.

"Did you look at the help-wanted ads today, Simon?" she asked without looking up.

"I'm making some calls this afternoon."

"Better get on it. Or your father could find you something at the store."

"I'll find something," Simon said. "If I have to."

"You can do what you want," she said, "but if you want to drive, you'll have to chip in for the insurance."

"But Mom, I have my whole summer planned. I'm at the gym every morning, the cages and field every afternoon. I'm trying to plan for my *future*."

"Which is fine, and I applaud your dedication. But you have to also provide for the present."

"It'll *totally* ruin my training."

She smiled. "I'm sorry, sweetie." Then she turned back to the pile of mail. "Solve your problem however you want. But if you want to drive, you'll need to start earning some money. We don't have a lot of that to go around."

"No kidding," Simon mumbled.

Near the bottom of the pile, she paused at a letter from the college. As she flipped it over to open it, Danny noticed that it was addressed to her.

She pulled out a packet of information and put it beside her, turning first to the letter. She read it quickly, then smiled and read it again a bit more slowly, her eyes moving back and forth and beginning to shine. Danny watched her carefully, but it wasn't the mad-scientist shine he'd seen earlier. This was something else.

"Well, children," she said, "I have some great news."

Bridget had just put a wedge of apple into her mouth. "What is it?" she said, quickly wiping a little stream of juice from her chin.

But that was as far as she got.

It was strange how it began. It wasn't like the time when the television exploded. That had happened very quickly—a sharp crackle and a loud smashing sound as the tube shattered in the living room. This happened much more slowly. At first the sound was actually quiet, too quiet to interrupt a conversation, except that it was the most unusual sound any of them had ever heard. Something outside started popping in short, almost clicking sounds, like a cap-gun fight between Alvin and his chipmunk friends. Everyone in the kitchen stopped talking, stopped chewing, stopped moving and just listened. Then, as if they'd been given a signal, they all jumped up and ran to the back door to see what was happening.

Before they made it, there was a tremendous explosion, like the sound of a gigantic door slamming on the world. *Boom!* Bridget screamed. Danny jumped about ten feet in the air as their mother shouted, "Ohmygod!" He started to run to the window, but Bridget had reached out and grabbed Danny's arm, squeezing it so hard it hurt.

"Get back in the kitchen right now!" their mother shouted. She was shaking. "Now stay right there, do you hear?"

The three of them nodded and followed her onto the porch.

A huge black cloud rose up through the trees. Flames

and more smoke leapt and billowed in the stand of trees where the shed had once stood. It looked as if a bomb had been dropped in the middle of the yard. But it wasn't that.

The shed had exploded.

Danny watched, amazed, as the shed continued to burn and pop and crackle. Burning pieces flew out of the flames, screaming and whistling and then exploding about thirty feet away. Balls of light and color launched themselves from the smoking ruin. It was like nothing they'd ever seen before, and Danny couldn't take his eyes from it.

But he felt someone staring at him, and when he turned, Bridget grabbed him again by the arm. "You touched it, Danny," she said. Her eyes narrowed and she let her glasses slide way down to the tip of her nose. "You touched it."

"Touched what?"

"You know perfectly well what. The formula. You touched the formula. On chaos theory?"

"So?"

"So *look*!" she said, pointing to the yard. "It's just like with Grampa Joe," she whispered.

The thought sent a shiver down Danny's spine, but he tried very hard to push the idea from his mind. How could he be responsible for the shed's exploding? How could *touching* something make it real? No, it had to be something else.

Danny turned from Bridget's glare and looked at his mother. She stood leaning against the porch railing, and suddenly her hand went to her forehead and she looked as if she'd just slipped on a patch of ice. She ran into the kitchen. Danny watched her through the door. She grabbed an envelope from the pile of mail and a pencil off the hutch. Standing hunched over the paper, she wrote without stopping for several minutes. She checked her work slowly and then set the pencil down. When she walked through the door and back onto the porch, Danny turned to Bridget. "Look at Mom," he whispered.

By the time she returned to the porch, the mad-scientist look had returned and she was clutching the scrap of envelope to her chest and staring at the shed but seeing somewhere beyond it.

"Wade?" she whispered.

At first, Danny didn't see his father. But then he saw that the van was in the driveway where his father always parked it, and as he peered through the smoke, he saw that his father was standing in the middle of the driveway. How many times had Danny seen him arrive home from work, close the van door gently, then turn and walk slowly along the gravel driveway? And every time, just before he reached the porch, he'd stop and look up, rub the top of his head, and sigh.

The explosion had clearly taken him by surprise. His body was facing in the direction of the house, but his head was turned to the shed, which exploded in reds and blues right in front of him. He was close enough to the shed that sparks landed at his feet and on his arms. But he didn't move, and Danny could see that his eyes were closed and his head slightly raised.

He wore his work uniform—the hunter-green coveralls

emblazoned with a bright orange SuperValu logo on the chest. Opposite the logo, his name was stitched in white cursive letters, the kind you see on bowling shirts. His bald head shone in the afternoon sun and reflected the flash of fire and light from the burning shed.

Standing like that, turned toward the house but facing the burning shed, he looked like a man trapped between things. Danny stared at his father's smooth, shiny head and his green coveralls, and thought of the name Simon had given their father: the Cuke. Simon had said it with such disdain. And then, the way he often did, he'd laughed it off. The Cuke. Some joke.

But what surprised Danny was how, as soon as the name had been spoken, it fit his father *perfectly*. He did in fact look just like a cucumber, in shape and color. But now Danny saw the other way in which his father was just like a cucumber. He seemed stuck, like a squash tethered to a vine in the garden. He worked a job he didn't like. The family farm he'd inherited was falling down around them—and in this case, literally *exploding* before their eyes. And he seemed powerless to change any of it, in the same way a cucumber is a cucumber and can't do anything about the condition of the garden. The Cuke. It fit.

And the worst part of all was that as Danny stared at his long, green, bald father, all he could think about were the countless times people had said to him, "You're the spitting image of your father." Was it true? He did look like him—except for the balding part. But what about the other part? Was Danny as helpless as his father seemed to be? The suggestion made him angry, probably because, down deep, it felt true. And then he heard Simon's favorite nickname for him in his ears, cruel and cutting. Simon called him the Pickle.

It was true. And he suddenly felt that he and his father were linked, destined to live the same miserable life. Was there no way to escape it?

He turned and looked at his mother.

She stared at her husband but spoke to Bridget. "Call the fire department, please, Bridget." Then she called out, "Wade, come away from the fire."

He looked startled, but slowly turned and, wiping soot and smoke from his sleeves, walked toward them.

"Claire," he said. "Are you, are the kids—"

"We're fine," she said.

"Good."

Bridget came back onto the porch. "The fire department is on the way."

"You called," their father said. "That's a good idea. Do you think we should get the hose or something?"

"I think we should wait," Claire said.

"That makes sense." He turned and looked at the fire. "Do we know what happened?"

"The shed blew up," Simon said.

His mother shot him a warning glance and Bridget mumbled, "Thank you, Sherlock."

"I don't know what happened," their mother answered. "We were having lunch and . . ."

"And *boom!*" Simon said.

His mother shot him another look. "That's enough, young man."

Their father still stood in the driveway. He rubbed his head and spoke slowly, as if he'd just come out of a dream. "Your lab," he said. "It's ruined, Claire. What are we going to do?"

"Oh, I'll figure something out. I'm just glad we're safe."

"You were in there this morning when I left," he said. She nodded.

"Are you sure you're okay?" he asked.

"I'm fine." She looked at the flames. "But it's quite a mess."

"Yes," he said. "One more thing to be fixed." He sighed.

"What are you doing here?" she asked. "I thought you'd be at work."

He rubbed his head again and put his hands in his pockets. "I came home for lunch. I don't know why, really. Summer, everyone home. I just thought I'd surprise you."

"Looks like we all got surprised," she said.

He nodded his head slowly and, staring at the fire, said, "Just when I thought it couldn't get any worse . . ."

In the distance they could hear the wail of sirens, and Danny imagined firefighters rushing down the highway to save something that was already destroyed. They were traveling with hope, but his father's tone confirmed what he could already see. There wasn't anything to be hopeful about. The shed was gone.

And for some reason it felt like the shed was the least of it.

Danny could feel his mother stiffen beside him. "It's

not as bad as it seems, Wade," she said. "The shed was old and needed to be torn down anyway."

"I suppose so," he said. "But the work. Cleaning the site, rebuilding. And the money."

His mother sighed loudly. "Yes. It's a mess. It's all a mess. And I'll figure something out." Then she stormed off the porch to meet the fire engines.

"Are you sure you're all right, Claire?" his father asked as she passed him.

She turned to him, her back straight, her mouth a thin line in her face. "Yes, Wade, I'm fine. There's nothing you can do."

Fire engines pulled into the driveway and headed toward the smoke. The children watched as the hoses were unloaded and streams of water smothered what was already largely out anyway.

After the firefighters left, Danny and Bridget stood on the porch and watched their mother pick her way through the debris. She carried a plastic bucket with her and they listened to the plunk of ball bearings and the crunch of charred wood under her feet. She dug around for about an hour, slowly making her way through the mess. Suddenly she dropped her bucket and stooped in one spot, digging feverishly, picking up one thing after another until her hands were full. Then she stood and held them in the air. "They made it," she called to Danny and Bridget, smiling. "They made it."

She was holding her prisms.

4

The day after the shed exploded, Danny woke to the smell of burnt plastic and wood and a voice in his head that kept repeating, *You touched it. You touched it.* He opened his eyes and tried to make sense of what had happened the day before, but he couldn't.

He threw off his sheet and listened to the house. He could hear the quiet scraping of forks and knives on plates, and then, on the edges of the sharp tang of carbon, he smelled something else. Pancakes. It was Saturday.

He practically leapt from his bed, pulled on his shorts and shirt from the day before, and ran down the hall. All worries disappeared. Pancakes could have that effect on people.

In the kitchen, everyone was behaving as if nothing had happened. His father was making pancakes; his mother was sitting a little stiffly at the table, but she was drinking coffee and going through another stack of mail. Simon sat at the counter eating more than his share.

Danny's father was huddled over a pan of freshly poured batter, checking the bubbles as they formed and popped. "Good morning," he said as Danny walked into the kitchen.

Danny poked his head over the stove to smell the pancakes.

This was the weird thing about his dad, Danny thought. When Danny thought about him in a general way, his father was sort of boring. It wasn't that he hadn't done anything exciting or interesting. He had. He'd traveled in China and Tibet. He'd married a smart, beautiful woman. He'd lived a life that seemed to point him toward something.

And then something had happened. He'd gone from being a traveling adventurer to being the Cuke. He not only looked lost, he also looked as if he'd given up trying to find his way. He went to work with his hands in his pockets, and he came home with his hands in his pockets. He never talked about dreams. He never talked about the future at all.

And he looked sad all the time.

Except when he cooked.

Danny stared into the pan and remembered all the amazing things his father had done with food. On a regular basis he made dinners with exotic vegetable dishes that were so strange and wonderful that it was hard to tell if they were perfect or just bizarre. They were surprising and delicious and weird and mysterious. Eating his father's food was sometimes the strangest thing. It was as if the food became an experience all by itself.

Danny would often sit at the kitchen counter and watch him throw vegetables into pots and toss them with the most random things from the refrigerator and cupboards—milk and cloves, sour cream and blueberry wine vinegar, cocoa and soy sauce, a pinch of this spice and a shake of that one. And he wasn't limited to vegetables. On his parents' anniversary, Danny's dad would make flaming trout or flaming roast duck—something on fire because their mother loved a meal with a chemical reaction in it. And Danny had the sense, even at thirteen, that this was a very unusual thing indeed. The whole family knew it, and there was general consensus that, if he wanted to, his father could have sold those recipes to some of the best restaurants in the state.

But he never did. His family encouraged him to open a bakery, a diner, even set up a cart at the farmers' market, but he never did. Something stopped him, and no one could understand what.

Danny would often watch his father to find a clue that might help him understand this deep reluctance. His father would cook and stir, poke and taste, and in the end arrange plates that were almost too pretty, too interesting to eat. But Danny noticed that as soon as his father sat at the table, it all changed. He'd stare around the table and smile a little sadly, and even though everyone raved about his food, he looked as if the food on the table was inconsequential—as if all that he'd done, in the end, didn't really make much of a difference in the world. He looked, Danny often thought, like he'd failed, like he'd found something precious and fleeting and then immediately lost it again.

Danny grabbed a glass of milk and watched his father stir the pancake batter, taste it, add something to it. The way he worked with food was as extraordinary as the food he made. He just reached into places and pulled out bottles and cartons and carelessly tossed their contents into the pan or the pot. There was this sense of control and complete lack of control—the Cuke and the master chef blending and changing until you couldn't tell which was which as he stirred and tossed and tasted and smiled.

His way with breakfast foods in particular was legendary—almost mythical. There were family stories of soufflés so light, they hovered over the plates, held down only by the weight of the asparagus or cheese. There were the tales of homemade yogurts that tasted like custards, flavored with coffee and orange and vanilla and pears, so that when you tasted them for the first time, you had to hold the dollop on your tongue for five or ten seconds before you could bring yourself to swallow. They were almost addictive delights.

And then there was his banana bread.

The banana bread story was a family classic. It was the story of how Danny's parents met, a story of magic and destiny. And at the heart of it was the banana bread.

The story went like this: He was at Harvard studying chemistry and thinking of going into the wine business; she was at Radcliffe and already well regarded in the physics department. She was studying in the park when he passed by. He was thinking about fermentation processes when he saw the most beautiful woman in the world sitting on a bench. "The perfect bench," she would say, "with just the right mixture of shade and light"—and she'd organized her materials beside her, note cards just so, books and binders here, pencil case off to the side. "And I'd just begun reading a very important chapter from Max Planck's *Treatise on Thermodynamics*," she would add for Bridget's sake, when he literally stumbled upon her—stumbled *into* her, "like she was a magnet," he'd say.

And then his mother would smile and say, "And your father banged right into me and scattered my pencils, note cards, and books in a thousand directions across the grass and sidewalk. I should have seen it as a premonition, but that banana bread . . ."

That banana bread. The magic. That was how his father talked about it. The banana bread was magic.

Horrified by his own clumsiness, his father had dug out a piece of his homemade banana bread from his jacket pocket, got down on his knee, and offered it to her as an apology. "Take this, please," he'd said. And she would tell them how she had noticed the kindness in his eyes even before she noticed that his socks didn't match and his shirt collar was worn to tatters. "And that banana bread," their mother would say with her mouth full of the fresh loaf their father made for her every year at that time, "was just like this. Heavenly. How could I walk away from a bread like this?" They'd laugh and tell the children that they knew instantly, the moment the bread touched their lips, that this was love. They got married within a year. Just like that.

"And from that moment," their father always said, "our family began. Each of you is a natural extension of that love." And he'd hold out his arms, and when they were little, they'd all move close together and he'd wrap them up, pulling them into the story itself.

Danny had heard the story at least a dozen times, but every time was like the first time, and he listened as intently as if it was a ghost story or a magical story, which it kind of was.

But they hadn't had a "banana bread anniversary" in a while. Not for years.

Pancakes didn't have quite the same power, but they were amazing in their own right. Danny watched as his father shaped them into medieval weapons. His special trick was to use pistachio nuts as the heads of fallen victims or as large stones to be hurled. Danny stared at them with wonder. The weapons were completely different from the cute little animals his father sometimes made out of vegetables for dinner.

"No cute little pancake chipmunks this morning?" Danny asked.

His father smiled. "Furry woodland creatures are for dinner only."

"Why?"

"Because, my son, dinner is about making peace with the day. But breakfast," he said, dropping five or six pistachio bombs into the pan, "is about preparing for it, and things might get ugly."

Danny nodded. "You can say that again. Can I have a catapult?" Knowing the way things had been going, he thought some long-range weapons might come in handy.

"You may." His father smiled. "With a hurling pistachio, I presume?"

"Better make it three."

"Three it is," his father said. "The real fight, I'm sure, will be over who will devour the lance and battle-axe."

"I'll have another crossbow, if you have one," Simon said. He had syrup on his chin.

"Someday," Danny said, "you're going to have to teach me how you do this."

His father smiled again. "The secret, I suspect," he said as he flipped a crossbow onto Simon's plate, "is a lot like baseball. You find the zone and just go with it. Isn't that how it works?"

Simon nodded. "Pretty much."

"Is that how it works with the banana bread, too?" Danny asked.

"That," his father said, "is a mystery even to me. The banana bread is a baked prayer, my boy. Nothing short of divine inspiration in that loaf."

"Or some exotic banana liquor," Simon said, catching Danny's eye and laughing.

"No, sir," his father said. "Just plain old-fashioned magic."

Simon laughed.

"And what can I get for the young scientist?" their father

asked, turning to Bridget as she came into the kitchen. "Would you care for an implement of destruction, or would you rather something more civilized? Perhaps a theta or a pi?"

Bridget rubbed her eyes. She looked as if she'd been up most of the night. "A pi would be lovely, thank you, Dad," she said. She looked at Danny and mouthed the words "My. Room. Later."

He nodded.

"And Claire?"

"I'm not really in the mood for a siege," she said without looking up from a phone bill. "How about just a round one?"

Her husband smiled. "The perfect and eternal shape for the lovely lady."

Their mother said nothing. When he placed a plate of perfectly round cakes in front of her, she cut them quickly and gently applied syrup—a tablespoon's worth on top and on the side, just the way she always did.

Danny looked into the pan to monitor the progress of his catapult. His father took the batter and drew out a pancake shaped like a small table.

"That's the symbol for pi," his father explained. But when Danny still looked confused, his father whispered to him, "It represents a number used to figure out the size of circles and things like that."

"Oh, right. I knew that."

Bridget was staring at them. "You spell it *p-i,* and it's approximately equivalent to the value of twenty-two divided by seven."

"Thank you, super-genius eavesdropping person," Danny said.

"Any luck with summer jobs, Simon?" their mother asked as she flipped through the mail.

"It's been a little crazy around here since you last asked me," he said. "But I think I've got a lead on some landscaping."

"I can always put in a good word for you at the SuperValu."

"Thanks, Dad, but I think I'm all set." Simon looked at Danny quickly and pretended to put his finger down his throat. *Work with the Cuke? Gag me!*

Danny's father flipped the pancakes. "Any interesting mail this week?" he asked.

Danny suddenly remembered a letter from the college that had come yesterday.

But his mother didn't mention it. "Some bills we need to talk about. The Free Tibet Society asking for money. Really, Wade, is that necessary?"

"Well, I don't know about *necessary,* but it would be nice."

"What's it for?" Simon asked.

"A kind of penance, I guess," he said.

"What's a penance?"

Their mother shook her head and sighed. "And we call ourselves Catholics."

His father answered him without looking up from the pancakes. "It's a punishment for a sin."

"Did you commit a sin? Did you do something really bad?"

40

"Some sins," his father said, "are sins of omission."

"What's that?" Danny asked.

"A sin of omission is when you *should* do something good and truthful but you fail to do it."

"You didn't do something good?"

"Sort of."

Claire tossed the stack of bills onto the table and sighed.

"Pancakes are ready," their father said. Food had always been his favorite diversion.

"Speaking of sins of omission, this came for you." Their mother reached across the table to hand over an envelope.

Danny watched his father carefully as he opened the letter, read it, and smiled.

"What is it, Dad?"

"It's a letter from my old boss, Larry Chandler."

"Who's he?" Bridget asked.

"He ran a brewpub in Cambridge," their mother answered. "Your father worked for him while he was in school. He thought being a chemistry major and working at a brewery made it a work-study opportunity. He spent more time brewing beer than he spent in the chem lab."

Their father stared at the letter. "He says he's opening a new restaurant." He looked up at them. "Here in town."

"You're kidding," their mother said, her eyebrows raised.

"No. He said he's had enough of the franchise business. What was he into again?"

"Applebee's, I think."

"That's right. Well, he's made his millions, he says, and now he wants to do something original. Here in town, of all places. Can you believe it?"

"Why is he writing you about it?" she asked.

He put the letter down but continued to stare at it. "He wants me to be the head chef and brewmaster."

"Are you kidding?" she said, her voice rising with anticipation.

"No. That's what he says."

"Let me see that," she said, grabbing the letter. She read quickly, her face brightening. "Oh, my heaven, Wade. This is incredible."

"Yes, I guess it is."

"I mean it," she said. "Think about what this could mean for you. You've always loved cooking. You have a gift—we've all seen it. And now an opportunity to use it. This is amazing."

"Yeah, I guess it is."

"Did you see this part?" she said, pointing to the letter. "He says he doesn't even care what kind of restaurant you want to open. It can be anything. It's entirely up to you." She stared at him. "Wade. Do you know what this means?"

"It means we could serve pancakes and chutney if we wanted," he said.

She laughed.

"You could call it Breakfast Anytime," Bridget said. "Pancakes in the shape of medieval weapons or Renaissance musical instruments or modern-art replicas. You name the date, we'll name the cake."

"Timeless Eats," their father said, laughing.

"You could serve the banana bread and have a dating

service on the side," Simon said. "Danny might even try it out."

"Shut up, Simon," Danny said, but he was laughing. It seemed they hadn't laughed like that as a family for a long time.

Their father smiled and chuckled, but even as the laughter filled the room, he'd already turned back to the pan and was staring into it.

"So, are you going to respond?" their mother asked.

"Oh, I don't know," he said into the pan.

"Why not, Dad?" Danny said. "It sounds like a great idea."

"Restaurants are a lot of work, Danny. And it's a pretty huge risk."

Danny heard his mother sigh, and when he turned, he saw that she'd drawn her mouth into a straight line. "Don't do this, Wade," she said.

"Do what?"

"Just think about it," she said. "This might be a sign. Maybe things are changing for the better. Maybe this is what we've been waiting for."

He shook his head. "I don't know, Claire. Doors open and doors close. And in the end, well, I guess you tend your garden where it blooms."

"That sounds an awful lot like the advice an old friend gave you."

"Who are we talking about?" Bridget asked.

"*We,*" her mother said, pointing to her husband and herself, "are having a *private* conversation."

"At the breakfast table in front of your children," Bridget added.

"We're talking about my friend, Jerome," her father said. "My friend in the photograph in the living room."

"The one in Tibet?" Danny asked. "The one who died?"

"Yes."

"Why did he say that to you about the garden?" Bridget asked. "Did he know you had a garden?"

"He said it before I had a garden."

"Is that why you planted one?"

"That's a good question," Claire said. "Is that why you planted it? Did you think he was being literal, actually talking about a *garden*?"

"No. But it seemed to make sense at the time."

"I love that garden," Bridget said.

Clare looked hard at her husband. "That's not what he meant, you know."

"How do you know what he meant, Claire?"

"And he certainly didn't mean you should let life pass you by. He didn't mean you should give up everything because, for a period of your life, you chose a different path."

"It wasn't for a period of my life. It *became* my life."

"Only if you say it's your life."

"It's not that simple."

She sighed. "You are a genius with food. Can't you see that? And you were on your way to doing something extraordinary. Remember the offer you had at that vineyard in Napa; the job you could have gotten with the Sam Adams Brewing Company? Then you went off to Tibet for a summer, came back, and gave it all up. I remember how excited you were when you returned. You were saying all those crazy things that Jerome told you—about being the water and tending a garden, and the other one about finding order in the chaos—but over time they all seemed to lose meaning for you. And now, twelve years later, you earn twelve-fifty an hour at the local grocery store. Is *that* how you thought it would work out, Wade? Is that what Jerome sent you back for? Is it? Is that the dream you had when I first met you?"

"It's the way things *are*."

"And that's it? All done? For us both? I have to keep my job typing grant proposals for professors who are half as smart as I am?"

"I'm just saying that doors close, Claire. Doors close."

Simon pointed to the letter in his father's hand. "Didn't that door just open? Think about it, Dad. You could open a restaurant near the college. College kids love pancakes and beer, everybody knows that. It could be perfect."

"You could wear normal clothes to work," Danny added.

His father laughed, but Danny could tell that he was suddenly different. The cooking Dad had gone, and although he stood with a spatula in his hand next to a griddle full of pancakes, he was the Cuke again. He laughed, but it was a sad laugh. It was the laugh Danny was used to hearing.

"It's not that easy," he said. "And this isn't an open door. It's just a kind note from an old friend. Nothing else."

"It's nothing else if that's what you *want* it to be," his wife said.

"That's all it *is*, Claire. That's all it is."

45

"Can't you open your own doors?" Danny asked.

"No, Danny, I don't think you can."

"But you can knock, Wade Parsons," their mother said, rising from her seat. "You can knock." She gathered her dishes and walked with them to the sink. She had cut into her pancakes but hadn't eaten any, so that the circles lay broken and dark with syrup. She turned to her husband. "There's a difference between making a place for yourself in the world and having a place made for you. You can tend your garden where it blooms, but that doesn't mean you can't plant what you want."

"I'm happy," he said, staring into the pan.

"Are you?" she asked. "Or are you afraid?" She put her dishes into the sink without looking at them. She stared hard at her husband. "What if a closing door is just fear? What if that's all it is?"

When he didn't answer, she quietly walked out of the kitchen.

Still holding his spatula, Danny's father turned and stared at his children.

Danny couldn't look at him. He'd never seen him look more like the Cuke before. And the worst part about it was that he *let* himself be the Cuke. He *chose* that.

"More pancakes?" his father asked.

But no one wanted more.

5

Right after breakfast, Simon left for the baseball field. He invited Danny to come along, shag some balls, take some swings. The field was next to Sarah Evans's house, and Danny found himself longing to go, maybe see her. But if he did, what then? What would he say to her? What did he *ever* say to her? Nothing. He sat behind her in three of his classes, could hardly breathe when she was near him, and had *never* said anything to her. Ever. If he saw her at the field, he might wave or say hi, but that might be even worse. What if she thought he was weird? What if she laughed at him every time he fell asleep in algebra and his books slid off his desk onto the floor? What if she was just like everybody else in school? No, he wouldn't go to the field. Something about his parents' argument helped him see himself as Sarah Evans probably saw him, and he didn't like it much.

"You sure?" Simon asked.

"Yeah. I just feel like staying home."

"Okay. That probably works out for Bridget, too. Now she can keep calling you Big Bang Boy, which she seems to enjoy."

"Very funny."

"What's up with the name, anyway?"

"Nothing. Bridget's an idiot, that's all."

Simon nodded. "Whatever. Stay if you want. I'll see you later."

The screen door slammed behind him.

Danny knew that Bridget wanted to see him, but the Big Bang Boy thing made him mad. He deliberately avoided her and instead snuck to his room. What he needed was a good dream, a moment when everything made sense. A dream was the answer, and his bedroom was the best place to make it happen.

Danny had made his room into a library of information about world cultures and histories. To prepare for a good dream, he first spent about ten minutes staring at maps of the continents and detailed maps of major cities of the world that covered most of two walls. Around them hung larger collages of photos from each region, and he let his eyes and his mind wander over photographs of a Mayan temple from Central America, an ancient Peruvian village from South America. He looked at a picture of a camel in the desert in northern Africa, reindeer herds, igloos, palaces from Arctic regions and the Far East. He had collected maps and travel bureau promotions from the Caribbean, the Middle East, European cities like Prague and Venice, Córdoba and Nice, Split and Bruges, and the possible lives opened up before him.

It was like a refuge, and he closed his eyes and breathed. A dream. A life. To be somebody else, anybody else, anybody at *all.*

He spent all morning and into early afternoon on the floor of his room, trying to dream up a life that would make him feel more like himself. But something was wrong. The dreams weren't working out the way he expected.

The first weird thing about his dreams was that his father always died suddenly in a freak accident.

The second weird thing was that tragedy always struck him down right as his new life was about to take off. And his collapse always involved pickles.

This was very alarming. For years Simon had been calling Danny the Pickle in those moments of meanness that came over him now and again, but never had that name—and the associations connected with it—invaded his dream world. His dreams had always been the place where he could escape it.

Until now.

Still, he had hope, and he lay on the floor, breathing, clearing his mind, and waiting for one more dream to take him. One more try. This one will be right. His eyes followed a long crack in the ceiling. It was the shape of the Snake River in Colorado, and it ran from the light in the center of the ceiling to the window behind him. He could feel the sun creep along the floor, now touching his feet, now his shins. He breathed in the smell of the drying soil in the garden and the fresh-cut grass, which Simon had mown the day before.

And then he could see it.

He can hear the sharp clanking of iron on iron and the hiss of pressurized steam. He is the second son of a railroad tycoon from Colorado. His father owns lines running all over the West, and he longs to ride the rails his whole life. But then his father dies in a freak cattle stampede. The two sons split the railroad line at the Continental Divide and the thirty-ninth parallel. The older son is young and strong and a respected baseball player. He sees a future in coal and builds his line with a concentration on container cars. Danny, who inherited his father's nose and jaw but none of his business sense, puts his money on tourism and builds a railroad of coach cars. He holds a ribbon-cutting ceremony marking the start of the new luxury service from Denver to San Francisco. The photograph in the paper shows the two brothers, their arms around each other, smiling. Simon is taller, his hand large on Danny's shoulder. The future looks bright.

And then it came. Danny, in a moment of insanity that feels strangely like genius, decides to limit rail concessions to a single item. He will sell only pickles. It is a disastrous choice. Why couldn't he have chosen pretzels? Cake? Meatball sandwiches? Why couldn't he have seen the good sense of going into the container business and followed Simon? Anything but pickles. People never want pickles. So they stop booking fares. They take buses instead. They hitchhike. Railroad business plummets. A change needs to be made, and soon. But Danny, paralyzed by choice, just keeps carrying pickles, to the great detriment of the railroad. The pickles wind up costing the company millions. Hundreds of railroad employees lose their jobs. The railroad union is unforgiving. A week later, Denver officials find Danny beaten and naked outside his brother's home, his *nose and his jaw broken, his face swollen beyond recognition. But no charges are ever filed.*

"Why are you lying on the floor? I thought you were coming to my room."

Danny opened his eyes and stared up at Bridget. He moved his tongue around in his mouth and tried to focus. Every muscle in his body ached from the dream beating. "I was asleep," he mumbled.

"I've been waiting for you. Are you sick?" she asked.

He closed his eyes. "Sort of."

"You look like some stranger just told you that you look like your father," she said.

He rolled into a sitting position and faced her. Bridget held a book across her chest. She was wearing shorts and an "E=mc²" T-shirt. Her glasses had slid down her nose once again. They were too big for her face, but she insisted that that was why she liked them. She didn't want a pair that looked as if they *belonged* there. She'd never get rid of them if that were the case, and she planned to get rid of them as soon as their parents could afford contacts.

"Do you believe character is destiny?" he asked.

"I don't know," she said. "What does that mean?"

"You know, that your character or your personality sort of sets you up to be a certain person, to have a certain kind of job or live a certain kind of life."

"Yeah, I guess I believe that. I mean, I'm a girl, but I'm also a scientist, so even though I'm, you know, girly—"

"You're not really that girly."

"I know, but I might *become* more girly. Anyway, my

point is that even though I'm girly, I'm also a scientist, so I want to figure stuff out, find answers, solve problems."

"Mom's like that, isn't she?"

"I think so. Sometimes too much like that."

He nodded.

"So what are you thinking about?" she asked.

"Nothing. It's just, the other day, I was sitting in the living room, not really thinking, just, I don't know, listening to the house. Have you ever done that?"

She just stared at him. No other response necessary.

"Well, it's cool, in a way, and I was just listening to the house when Mom came in and asked what I was doing."

"What did you tell her?"

"That I was listening to the house."

"Bad answer."

"No kidding. So then she asked what I was thinking about."

"You didn't say, 'Nothing,' did you?"

He nodded.

"*Very* bad answer."

"Right. So then she just stared at me and then she said, 'It's not really your fault, you know.' What's *that* supposed to mean?"

But he knew what it meant. And even when Bridget shrugged, he knew that *she* knew what it meant, too.

"If character is destiny," he said, "I'm toast."

"Characters are complicated things," she said. "And sometimes they change."

"When?" he asked. "When do they change?"

"I don't know," she said. "When they *have* to, I guess." She leaned over to scratch her leg, and her hair, an enormous, tangled mass of red, fell across her face. It was curly and frizzy—like their father's sister, June's—although Bridget's looked like it hadn't been brushed in days. There were small pieces of twigs and burrs stuck in it. Then Danny noticed that her legs were covered in scratches, some of which were actually bleeding.

"Been doing some reading?" he asked, nodding not at the book, but at her legs.

"It's such a good book," she said, "and then suddenly I was standing in the middle of the Campbells' blackberry patch."

"That's half a mile from here."

"So?"

"So, have you ever thought that it might be safer to read sitting down in a locked room?"

"Very funny," she said, rubbing at the scratches on her other thigh. "It's not like I can *help* it, you know. Character is destiny."

That was true. They all could tell stories about Bridget's strange habit of walking while she read. Once, their father had to bring her home from Hudson State Park—ten miles away—because Bridget had gotten sucked into a book on something called Maxwell's Demon and had walked all the way there. They'd tried everything, but she couldn't stop. So they just added Bridget's habit to the long list of weird things about the Parsons family.

Danny felt the heat from outside fill the room, and he

suddenly wished they could head to the pool. *It could be that he is the second son of a Polynesian pearl diver who, when his father dies in a freak oyster accident, inherits—*

"Do you think it's weird that, all of a sudden, I keep dreaming that Dad dies?"

She pushed a clump of hair behind her ear. "Not really. It's probably a phase of adolescence or something."

He thought about this. "Yeah, that makes sense." He nodded at her book. "So what are you reading?" he asked.

"You wouldn't like it."

"Why not?"

"It's about a guy who goes around solving math problems, getting rich, doing good stuff like that. But with math."

Danny wrinkled his nose. "People can actually get rich that way?"

She smiled. "Only in Pakistan, I think."

"Figures." His eyes glazed over for a moment. "Of course," he mumbled, "if you were *the second son of a great sultan, then—*"

"Hey, Big Bang Boy."

Her voice startled him. "What?"

"You're doing it again."

There were the hallway mirror and the window by the stairs. His bedroom door. He could smell the sharp pang of charred wood and burnt plastic from the shed. He wasn't in Pakistan. He wasn't even close. "Sorry," he said. "And if you call me that name again, I'm going to kill you."

Bridget laughed and rubbed the scratch on her thigh again and stared at her brother. "Speaking of Big Bangs,"

she said, "there's something I want to give you." Then she paused and her voice was suddenly serious, more serious than it almost ever was. "But I need to explain it first."

"A present?" He imagined a collapsible kung fu star, night-vision sunglasses, or an exploding cuff link.

"Not exactly. Come on. I'll show you."

He followed her—again!—into her room. He looked for a place to sit, even a place to step where he wouldn't be on top of something, but decided to stay in the doorway. "So what is it?"

"This," she said, and she turned from her desk to hand him a piece of paper.

He smiled at her from the doorway and waved.

"Aren't you coming in?" she asked.

"Where should I step?"

She clenched her jaw and groaned. Then she walked the paper across the room to him.

He looked at it without taking it. "It looks like a math problem."

"It is. That's what I have to explain." She pointed to her bed. "Sit down, it might take a while."

"Sit where?"

"On the bed. Anywhere. I don't care. Sit wherever you want."

"I want to sit in *my* room."

"Danny!"

"Okay, okay." He kicked aside a pair of jeans, a beach towel, three socks, and an empty box of graham crackers to make a path to Bridget's bed. Once there, he picked up a

pair of shorts and an old tennis shoe that was quickly losing its sole—the heel flapped at him as he held it at arm's length and dropped it onto the floor. Just before he sat down, he dug a half-eaten bag of Fritos from the foot of the bed, where it had become wedged against the frame, and tossed it onto the floor with the other things. At last, he slapped at the cleared space on the comforter to knock the largest crumbs to the floor and then carefully shimmied onto the clean spot without touching anything else.

Bridget stared at him.

"Don't look at me like that," he protested. "I found a piece of carrot cake on your desk the other day—it was under that February issue of *National Geographic* that I'd been looking for, by the way—and it had enough mold on it to be its own ecosystem. You're a pig, B. I've heard Mom say that she won't even walk *past* your room without arming herself with a can of Lysol and putting on her boots."

"She was joking."

"I don't think so."

Bridget paused. "Why boots?"

He raised his eyebrows doubtfully. "You have mice."

"*Had* mice."

"Fine. You *had* mice. Same thing."

Danny sat silently. It wasn't a conversation he wanted to have with Bridget, because it reminded him of the droppings they'd found collecting under Bridget's rug and *pillow*. His stomach turned just thinking about it. He changed the subject by nodding at the paper that Bridget still held in her hand. "Want to tell me what that is?"

"It's an experiment." She looked at the sheet as if she were working out the formulas in her mind.

"What are you going to do with it?" Danny asked.

"I want you to just hold it. You know, carry it around with you."

"Why?"

She stared at him hard and her eyes narrowed as she adjusted her glasses. It was the look of interrogation, the look that swears to find out the truth *no matter what.* Danny stared back for a moment, but then he looked away. "It blew up, Danny," she said finally. "You touched the formula and it blew up."

"I wish you'd stop saying that. The fire marshal said it was probably due to heat and poorly sealed gas cans. That and some fireworks—which I had nothing to do with."

"When people don't understand something, they come up with whatever explanation makes sense to them."

"Occam's razor," Danny said. "It's the theory that says that the simplest solution is probably the most accurate."

"That's not what it means," she said. "It means that one should not make more assumptions than the minimum needed. But nice try. And how did you learn *anything* about Occam's razor in the first place?"

Danny smiled. "I'm not as dumb as *some* people think."

She smiled. "But almost. And anyway, that doesn't prove that you're innocent, either."

"It doesn't prove that I'm guilty."

"But this might," she said, holding up the paper and waving it at him.

He rolled his eyes. "So what's your hypothesis?"

She smiled. "You used another science word. Good for you!"

"Very funny," he said. "So? Your theory?"

She stopped smiling. "I think you can do it again."

"How will you prove it?"

She handed him the paper. "Just carry this around. That's all you have to do. Carry this around and let's see what happens. If I'm right, then we should see some change. If I'm right, this formula will *happen,* just like the other one did."

"Are you kidding?"

She shook her head.

Danny rolled his eyes again. It was ridiculous, it really was, but he'd show her. "Fine. Give me the stupid paper."

Bridget smiled. But she didn't give the paper to him just yet. "Don't you even want to know what it is?" she asked.

"Not really." Something in his mind told him that the less he knew, the better. But why? It didn't make sense. He hadn't known what the formula in the shed was about. Or had he? No, he hadn't known but he had *imagined* that he knew. Did knowing make a difference? "Should I?"

"I would," Bridget said in that offhanded way of hers, but she was watching him carefully. *She's begging,* he thought. *In her own way, she's begging me to ask.*

"Well," he said, curiosity getting the best of him, "what is it?"

Bridget smiled cautiously. "Are you sure?"

"Just tell me before I change my mind." Because down

deep, he really *didn't* want to know. But he didn't want *her* to know that.

"What if I tell you and *then* you change your mind?"

"Won't happen."

"Promise?"

"Just tell me!"

"Okay. There was a group of scientists," she began, but then she stopped. "You don't really want to hear this, do you?"

It was strange how, as soon as he heard the word *scientists,* his eyes had started to glaze over. It was the kind of thing that happened to him all the time in school. "I'm thinking maybe you should stick to the main topic."

She smiled. "Okay, the main topic," she said. "That formula in the shed was about entropy, remember? And entropy measures the extent that the universe is always moving toward disorder. Paint eventually starts to chip, plants rot, metal stuff rusts. And energy is needed to bring things back into order. But there's a finite amount of usable energy in the universe and every time we fight chaos we use some of it. The fact is that someday we'll run out of usable energy and everything will be chaos. And that's what the math formula that Mom was working on proves."

Chaos theory. Entropy. But he had imagined it was about spontaneous combustion.

"So you think I unleashed chaos—or entropy—on the world? I thought you were smarter than that."

"Luckily for you, I'm a genius." She smiled again, and this time Danny found it impossible not to smile back. The fact was that Bridget *was* a genius, everyone said so. And her ridiculously high IQ was only half of it. She'd tutored Simon through chemistry and precalculus so that he wouldn't fail and lose his eligibility during baseball season. She read science journals and actually had e-mail conversations with the scientists about their findings. She was smarter than anybody. And like her mother, she dreamed of becoming a physicist.

"So what's *this* equation?" he asked.

She stared at him. "That one explains one of the most central proofs of quantum theory. Are you sure you want to know what it's about?"

That was like a doctor asking if you wanted to know the ugly details of the very painful procedure he was about to perform on you. If Bridget's theory was right, it was entirely possible that this could be very painful. "No, not really," Danny said. Then he paused. "It's not *very* dangerous, is it?"

"Not very."

He gave her a fake smile. "That makes me feel better."

"You don't have to do it."

"How will you know if your hypothesis is correct?"

She paused. "I'm not sure. But *you* should notice a difference. Maybe things around you will look different. Or you'll feel like there are moments when you aren't where you're supposed to be."

"That actually sounds completely dangerous."

"I doubt it. But if you're afraid to take it, then I guess that will prove my hypothesis as well."

"How?"

"Why would you be afraid to take something you knew

wouldn't work? You'd only be afraid to take something you knew *would* work."

"You think you're pretty clever, don't you?" He held out his hand. "Just give it to me."

As Bridget leaned toward him, Danny had the strangest feeling. It was the way he felt sometimes when he was in school and he could hear Mrs. Ferguson droning on about square roots and still be in a dream—that weird overlapping sensation of being in two places at the same time and not being entirely sure which one was real. Bridget held out the paper, but it wasn't Bridget, exactly. It was a girl he'd never seen before and she was handing him a flyer, a kind of advertisement with an address on it. "Go there," she whispered.

"There you go," Bridget said, and she handed him the paper.

Danny blinked, then took the sheet of paper. The edge was jagged, as if she'd just torn it out of her school notebook. He plucked at the nubs of paper along the edge as he stared at the figures. "So, what," he said, "you just made up this equation this morning, Miss Genius Person?"

"No. I actually got it out of this book." She reached behind her and grabbed a very thick book titled *Theories of Relativity*.

"Very clever."

"Sometimes being a genius means knowing where to *look* for answers."

Danny stared at the paper, at the numbers and symbols. Then he folded it carefully and tucked it into his back pocket.

"So that's it?" he asked.

"Just carry it around. See what happens."

See what happens. For some reason the words were almost terrorizing for Danny. It felt like he'd been given a ticking box. Just carry it around. See what happens.

"And if something *does* happen," Bridget said, "well, then we'll know, won't we? About the shed."

"I guess."

Danny stood and felt the folded sheet of paper move in his pocket. But something felt strange. Not physically, really. It wasn't the paper or a sense of foreboding. It was more like the way he felt the day he went to school when it had been canceled—the feeling of being in the wrong place at the wrong time. He slid off the bed and stepped carefully over the piles on the floor, but the closer he got to the door, the stranger he felt. It was almost like déjà vu, as if everything that was happening had happened before— or that it was never supposed to happen.

He was in the hall when the feeling became almost unbearable. Suddenly panicked about the paper in his pocket, he turned and called, "Bridget?"

But Bridget wasn't there. In fact, he was at the opposite end of the hallway. He remembered leaving her room, but he wasn't even near her room now. He was near his own room. He called her name again and was just about to begin to search for her in earnest. He called downstairs. He even looked out the window in his bedroom to see if she was somehow outside. But there was nothing. It was as if she'd just disappeared.

"What's going on?" he mumbled to himself. He reached into his pocket and pulled out the sheet of paper. He unfolded it and stared. There were marks across it, strange letters that spelled words that didn't make sense. It didn't look like the kind of equations Bridget wrote. It wasn't even in her handwriting. In fact, the more he studied it, the more convinced he became that the words were written in Russian. And there were pictures of crudely drawn elephants in the corner. Was it a circus ad? "What's going on?"

Then, from the open window in his room, he heard a strange noise coming from the barn. It sounded like someone was breaking small, dry boards. The air rang with sharp snapping sounds.

He put the sheet of paper back into his pocket, where it seemed to throb. Something very strange was happening. Was he experiencing the general theory of relativity, as Bridget had hypothesized? Or was it something else?

The memory of a snippet of a dream—a dark girl handing him a piece of paper and the words "Go there"— echoed in his head. Which was it? He needed to find out.

He ran down the stairs. The house felt utterly empty, but he tried to ignore the feeling he had of being completely alone. He tried to ignore the rising panic in his chest. He walked quickly and deliberately to the barn as if led by the sharp, loud sounds that seemed to whisper, "Go there." He walked as if there were nowhere else to go.

6

The barn smelled dank and musky, though it hadn't housed a farm animal in decades. They'd found a raccoon family in there once, and there were always mice and bats and swallows hiding in the darkest corners or the highest rafters. But the errant wildlife could never displace the sweet smell of cows and horses that seemed a part of the wood itself.

It was a large, whitewashed, old-fashioned barn with animal stalls and a huge hayloft. Danny's grandfather had kept brown quarter horses, and there was still a collection of riding tackle and an old brittle saddle in one of the storage rooms. But for at least ten years the barn had been empty of animals. They stored gardening supplies, fertilizers, tools, and seeds in a few empty stalls, some abandoned wooden furniture in another, and an old riding mower in the center corridor. Upstairs were about a dozen bales of straw that no one quite knew what to do with.

It was from the loft amid the abandoned bales that Danny had heard the noise.

As he neared the barn, Danny thought someone was smashing the stalls with a large hammer. A high whistle was quickly followed by a crack so loud, it made him jump. But once inside the barn, he knew it wasn't a hammer at all. It was something else.

There was only one way into the loft, and that was by climbing a narrow ladder at the far end of the barn. Danny climbed carefully. The rungs creaked like aching muscles.

It was dark in the loft, the light filtering through the spaces between the slats in the barn walls, and when he poked his head through the floor at the top of the ladder, he could barely see a figure at the far end of the barn walking into the patches of dust and darkness. It looked like his father, but all Danny could see with perfect clarity was the hazy glare that reflected off his glasses and hid his eyes. It was as if everything else had been sucked into the dust and darkness.

But if this was his father, something was different. This man wasn't dressed in the hunter-green work uniform with his name stitched over the pocket and "SuperValu" on the back in bold maroon and white letters. This man was wearing a loose shirt and a pair of khakis. It was an outfit Danny remembered seeing in a photo in the living room: his father, dressed just like this, with his arm around a bearded man about the same age, his friend Jerome. Behind them were some of the biggest mountains Danny had ever seen. The Himalayas.

What surprised Danny most of all was the fact that the man walking in front of him was barefoot, just like the man in the picture. And, with the exception of that picture, he couldn't ever remember seeing his father without shoes on.

Danny lifted himself as silently as he could onto the floor of the loft and sat on the closest bale of straw he could find. Ancient strands of straw dug into his leg, and Bridget's formula—or the paper, anyway—rustled in his pocket when he moved. He reached back to tuck it in and was alarmed to find that it was hot. He almost called out in surprise but caught himself in time. Whatever was happening in his pocket was very, very bizarre. But so was this whole situation. And in the end, there were just too many strange things happening to give his attention to all of them. One thing at a time. He left the paper alone.

His eyes slowly adjusted to the darkness, but something didn't feel right, and he almost stopped breathing, as if breathing might disturb whatever it was that was happening.

Gradually Danny was able to make out the figure that stood before him. It was, in fact, his father. He stood in the darkness, utterly still, his head raised slightly as if his eyes were closed. All around him, he'd placed empty soda cans on bales of straw and sawhorses, or he'd stuck them in the corners of rafter beams. Danny wasn't sure what the cans were for. He wasn't sure of anything—his father in the barn, the sounds of breaking boards.

And then he saw something that made him blink in disbelief. In his father's right hand was a gigantic bullwhip.

Danny tried to make himself as still as the figure that stood before him, but it was hard. His father looked like a statue. Danny couldn't even be sure he was breathing.

For almost five minutes nothing happened. Then his father raised his head and, with his eyes still closed, slowly moved his arms as if he were dancing. He raised his arms, lowered them, slowly moved his feet, and suddenly, without hesitation, he turned and began moving the whip back and forth, up and down, keeping rhythm to a silent tune. He spun and moved the whip all around as if it were a toy he was pulling through the air. And it moved as silently as he did, whispering through the air the way breath whispered from his mouth.

There was something careless about his movements, about the way his arm followed his body. Danny watched the whip. It seemed to come alive with energy, first growing tense and then organizing itself in a straight line that suddenly raced along the path of his father's arm until it sprang forth so quickly that Danny lost sight of it. Then his father's shoulders jerked slightly—a movement so casual, so quiet, that it seemed almost intuitive. His arm retracted and the whip snapped the air, exploded like a bottle rocket, and knocked a can off the sawhorse.

But that was just the beginning. Again, he slowly moved the whip, his eyes still closed, and then—*crack! Crack!*—he whirled and snapped one can after another until Danny lost count. He hit cans Danny never even saw. The last three he struck in rapid succession—*crackcrack-crack!*—so that all the cans lay on the floor around him.

Danny forgot himself and ran to pick up one of the cans. There was a sharp dent in its side, as though it had been struck by a nail.

Crouching in a blanket of straw, Danny stared back at his father. Dust particles swam around him, and the sun shining through the cracks directly behind him cast a ghostly glow about his shining head. He shimmered and seemed to nearly disappear, almost as if he'd become something from one of Danny's dreams. But Danny could see him gathering the whip in his hands, and when he looked up at him, he knew. His father was more than a produce man, more than just a father and husband. He was . . . he was a ninja.

His father turned slowly, bowed to the darkness, and then looked at Danny for the first time and smiled. "Have you been practicing?" he asked.

Danny froze. *Practicing?* he thought. *Practicing what?* But his father's smile tugged at him. "Uh," he mumbled, "not exactly."

His father's face hardened for a moment, but he forced a smile and said, "Come on, then." He held out the whip toward Danny. "Let's do it now."

Danny hesitated, but when his father jiggled the whip insistently, Danny walked to him and took the whip in his hands. It was a lot heavier than it looked.

And then it was as if he'd stepped out of his life completely and found himself in another life. It was just the way he'd imagined it—just the way he knew it would one day happen. He had become someone else. And his father was beside him, a different man, a man who—Danny suddenly realized—would lead him into a new life and make him the man he was meant to be.

Danny's father took him by the shoulders and moved him into the proper position.

Danny held the whip in his hand, lifting it gently, testing its weight. He watched it move up and down, its coils barely contracting, and then spring back into its natural shape. He'd never held anything with so much power and potential, never held anything that felt so alive and dangerous, and—how could he describe it?—almost hopeful.

Then he closed his eyes, just as he'd seen his father do.

His father stood behind him, guiding his arm with the whip, moving him as if they were part of some ancient dance. Danny felt the whip become an extension of him, and he heard his breathing grow slow and rhythmic until his breath mimicked the sound of the whip as it moved through the air. The whole barn fell into the rhythm of his breathing, in and out, in and out. And a strange sensation came over him, a kind of deep quiet that had nothing to do with the sounds of things.

Then his father left his side and, standing in the shadows, spoke to him.

"Energy," he said, almost breathlessly, "isn't something to be controlled. It's something to be ridden. Like a horse or like a wave. Energy is yours; you just have to find it and give it direction. Become the energy. Be the water and *use* its power."

Be the water. Danny had heard it so many times before, but never like this. Water equals power. He'd never thought of that. *Be the water.* And as the words echoed in his thoughts, his mind grew quieter and the piece of paper in his pocket slowly cooled.

"What we think we want," his father whispered, "and what we think we need are not the things we want and need. What we really want is energy. What we really want is to be the water because the water is a force we can *ride*."

Once again, he took Danny by the shoulders and squared him to the target can.

"Ride the energy," he whispered.

Afterward, Danny could never remember exactly what happened. He had begun to imagine that he was the second son of a Chinese farmer whose rich rice fields and enlightened spirit brought him great fame among his people, but the dream faded and his mind was empty. Empty.

And that was when it began. The movement of his arm, the whistling of the whip—he didn't feel or hear anything. But when he opened his eyes, he had hit a can.

He stared at the can, then at his father, who, unlike in every dream he'd had for the past week, stared back at him alive and well. There was a quiet light behind his eyes. Danny had hit a can. They both smiled.

It was all so much like a dream, the way his father smiled and spoke, the way Danny felt so in control of the world, so present. Usually he felt that his father was just *there*—like air or humidity or the sound of a plane flying twenty thousand feet overhead. He'd always just been there, and you could feel him and see him, but most of the time he was easy to forget.

But this Wade Parsons was different. He wasn't *opposite,* exactly. He was still the same man in important ways. He moved and spoke in the same way. His eyes were the same brown. If there was a difference, it was the difference between air and wind, the difference between energy and inertia. And that difference confused Danny to the point that he wondered if this actually *was* his father after all. If he hadn't known better, he would have thought that he'd stepped into a life he had up until then only imagined. But if it was an imagined life, it was more real than anything he'd ever imagined before. And it was so unlike his real life that he forgot for a moment that he *had* a real life.

"You hit them better than your brother, did you know that?"

"Simon?" Danny said, his mouth gaping open. The whip practically slipped from his hand.

"Yes," his father said. "Your brother's close. He's got a real gift—almost as powerful as yours." He paused and looked at Danny. "Are you okay, Dan?"

Danny readjusted his grip on the whip. "Yeah, sure," he mumbled. Dan. His father'd called him Dan. As if he were a man or something. "Simon does this?" he asked again, because it felt unreal to him to hear Simon's name, to hear that he was a part of this, *his* dream.

And it had to be a dream, didn't it? He felt as if he'd stepped into an impossible new life complete with a new father. An incredible life of whips and cans and power. He'd stumbled into the perfect life. It felt impossible that he might have to share it with Simon.

"Simon once hit ten cans in a row," his father was saying. "But it took him years to do that. He couldn't do anything with the whip the first time."

"Can anyone else do it?"

"Who else? Your mother?" He snorted—a sound that was half laughter and half anger—and looked away.

"What about Bridget?" Danny asked, speaking the name out loud—and more loudly than he'd intended—because it seemed so strange that his father hadn't already spoken it.

His father stared at him. "Who?"

Danny started to repeat the name, but stopped. He could tell from his father's expression that the name meant absolutely nothing to him. It was as if he had spoken the name of a stranger.

His father with the whip knew Simon and Danny, but he had no idea who Bridget was.

It was as if she didn't exist—as if she'd *never existed.*

"Who did you say?" his father repeated.

"Nothing," Danny said quickly. "Nobody. I was thinking of something else."

But there was a question racing through his head that he couldn't quiet. *Should I tell Bridget about this?*

Not a chance. Not yet.

7

Bridget sat in her room and listened for Danny. She'd given him the formula. And when he'd left, she'd listened for him. Would he go to his room? Downstairs? And what would happen now that he carried the power of mathematics in his pocket? Because it *was* power, wasn't it? She couldn't prove it, which bothered her, but she knew it was true. Danny had made the shed blow up. She just knew it.

But she didn't hear anything from the hallway. No closing doors, no footsteps on the stairs. It was as if Danny were standing motionless right outside her door.

Suddenly she felt the taste of panic in the back of her throat. She thought of Danny and the shed, the way his hands had just brushed the formula on the board. She'd handed him something just a moment ago that, contrary to what she'd told him, might put him in some danger.

She stepped out of her room, but the hallway was empty. She listened again. Nothing.

Something uncertain lay in the pit of her stomach. It felt like the moment before a difficult concept became clear, or the moment before she solved a proof that for days had felt impassable—that fluttering, elated, almost panicked feeling. Something was going on. Without thinking, she walked to Danny's room to find the answer.

Danny's room was immaculate compared to hers. Everything was in its place, but still, there was something sad about the room. It so clearly showed her the truth about him. If the shed was a symbol of their mother's deepest desire to become the physicist she almost was, then Danny's room was a symbol of his deepest desire to become, well, anybody but Danny Parsons.

On every wall, on every space in the entire room, was evidence of Danny's dreams. The magazines and notebooks, the maps and brochures—it all illustrated a different reality. And in the middle of all the maps and images of foreign worlds hung a small photograph of Danny. It was his seventh-grade class picture.

She lifted it slightly and found that there was another photo underneath. It was of Sarah Evans.

It struck her suddenly that there were so many things about him that she didn't know. All the things on the walls were only the surface of a private world that Danny hid in.

And yet, as Bridget stood in the middle of the room, ran her eyes across the maps and images and touched the spines of the notebooks and binders and magazines—there must have been almost two hundred of them—she thought, and not for the first time, about how similar she and Danny were.

Like Danny, Bridget also lived two lives that were almost completely separate. There was her regular life—the "real" world—where she got dressed and went to school, ate, brushed her teeth, helped Danny and Simon with their homework, and fed their rabbit, Bunserati. But the real world was really the most insignificant of Bridget's worlds. Most of her days were spent in the world of ideas, in the life of her mind.

Sometimes she felt like she had a disease, like narcolepsy—that disease where you can't stay awake. It was as if she were perpetually falling asleep and dreaming about ideas. And then Danny would knock on the door or her teacher would call on her and she'd suddenly wake up to the real world.

When she was little, people thought she had attention deficit disorder. She'd "wake up" and look confused, which she was. But over time she learned to compose her face more carefully. She learned to look directly at the face that spoke to her so that even if she had no idea what the person were talking about, at least she looked as if she were present and attentive. She learned to pick up clues. In school when she was called on, she'd quickly check the page that Billy Robinson was on. He always sat next to her and had a habit of pointing to the problem or question the class was discussing. She noticed what people carried, how they looked, the way they stood, so that she could mimic them even when she wasn't "there." She learned countless skills to help her compensate for the simple fact that most of the time she wasn't in the least interested in the real world.

She was interested in ideas—the ideas of science, theoretical mathematics, quantum and astrophysics. She was interested—ironic as it sometimes felt to her—in the ideas that formed the underpinning of the very reality that could never hold her interest.

But this wasn't the kind of interest that helps a girl make friends, and the fact was, Bridget had no friends. She never noticed the way Billy Robinson looked at her. She never noticed the fact that he was always behind her in the lunch line or behind her on the bus. She never noticed anything.

The strange part about this way of living was that it made her feel as if *she* were invisible. And people tended to confirm that perception. They talked about how smart she was, they talked about her future—all this talk *about* her. But nobody talked *to* her. And often, when she devoted a moment to thinking about her real life, she wondered what would happen if she weren't there. Who would notice? Who would care if the "spacey" kid just disappeared?

Sadly, she had to admit that probably nobody would care, except maybe her parents. Her father didn't *understand* her, really, but he loved her. Sometimes she thought he loved her best of all. She was the one he would always hug and check on after lights were out at night. Either he loved her best or he was working hard to *try* to love her best. But he didn't understand her. She was the daughter with gifts, and her father believed that gifts were burdens. He tended to downplay her abilities. He tried to make her feel "normal." He always said to her, "You should do what makes you happy," and "Go ahead and be a kid." It was as if he also heard the way people talked more about her *future* than about who she *was*. And that was something, even if it only served to emphasize that he, too, didn't know who she was.

And her mother would miss her because . . . well, because in a way they were the same. But her mother was almost the opposite of her father. She wanted Bridget to realize her potential, to make good choices. She wanted her to *become* someone happy. Her father wanted her to *be* happy. And there was a difference. Still, Bridget knew that her mother would be devastated to lose her. It was just that sometimes it felt as if what her mother would miss most was the *possibility* of Bridget, not Bridget herself.

Aside from her parents, though, there wasn't much else that made her *present*. It wasn't as if she was filling a hole in the world that would be revealed again without her there. No one would miss her in the big-picture way. No, she doubted anyone would really miss *her*.

Except Danny.

He would miss her most of all. Probably because, as she'd understood all along, she lived her life in exactly the same way he lived his.

Standing there before his maps and pictures, she knew that Danny's inner life was just as real as hers—perhaps even *more* real, because it was decorated with facts and details that *made* it real. Bridget's inner life had created chaos out of her real life, but Danny's had given his outer life order, and that order was everywhere apparent.

Bridget took down a notebook and marveled at the system Danny had developed for cataloging the lives he made up. She'd seen him work with it over the past year, but she'd never imagined how elaborate it had become for him. She marveled at the way he used the map over his bed to note his national identity with a colored pushpin and the way each pin would refer to a story of that life in a notebook of a corresponding color.

Bridget sat with several notebooks on her lap. At first she thought he'd organized the notebooks by country, which seemed the most logical way, but she found he'd organized them by the type of the lives he imagined. The blue notebook, for example, was titled "Royal Lives"—like the story of being taken from the family of the "dragon king" in Bhutan (his features surgically altered, of course), or of being swept from the bassinet of a Scottish laird.

The red notebook was called "Adventure and Intrigue"— he'd been the son of a KGB agent stationed in Berlin before his capture, or he'd been given this life when his father's ties to an elite CIA force were exposed to Iranian militants who were intent on killing them all.

He had a green notebook with no title that appeared to be for tales of wealth and influence. Bridget smiled as she imagined Danny turning to that notebook every time their mother delivered a pile of Simon's hand-me-down shirts and underwear to his room. In those stories he was to be the heir of great business empires—the son of a famous toy manufacturer in South Africa, or of a corporate finance mogul in Finland, or of a defense contractor hiding in the Galápagos Islands.

What Bridget never found was the orange notebook. Danny kept that one behind his old comic books in his desk drawer, hidden from the rest because it was different. The blue, red, and green notebooks played with a past that was lost, but the orange one was about the future—and not the exciting future that he had often imagined when he was in the shed. These futures felt to Danny more frightening, more possible, even inevitable. In that notebook he imagined that he was Danny Parsons after all. In it, he would write the story of the life that he thought he would most likely lead. They were frightful entries, if only because they seemed to come true as he put them down in words. He would grow up to be the manager of the produce department at the local SuperValu, and people would call him the Cuke, just as they had his father before him. He would always love a dark-haired girl from a distance. He would live in this room. He would care for his sick father. He would take a cruise in the Caribbean and would eat alone. He would fall asleep one night and have no dreams and never wake up again.

Later that night, after Bridget had left his room and the house was quiet, Danny would write a different story in the orange notebook. It was a story he wouldn't tell anyone about, because he both didn't understand it himself and knew that it was somehow already true. He would write about the moment he discovered that he possessed a special gift, a gift he couldn't control, a gift that might be able to give him anything he wanted in life, or a gift that might simply destroy everything that he loved. He would sit down and write for almost an hour, his hand flying over the page, his fingers cramping.

$$\text{\textcircled{A} \quad \textcircled{A} \quad \textcircled{A}}$$

Bridget spent that night reevaluating her experiment. She feared that something had gone wrong. The formula seemed harmless enough. Einstein's general theory of relativity was basically about objects in space. It defined the relationship between matter and space-time. She'd anticipated a change in time, or maybe in gravity: maybe Danny would get heavier, or lighter—maybe he'd start to *float*.

But at midnight she remembered something else about Einstein's general theory. On the one hand, it explains the general relation between matter and time and space, but on the other, it proves the existence of black holes—theoretical time-travel phenomena. And a black hole has two openings. Was it possible that Danny had touched the general theory of relativity, made a black hole in her bedroom, and then walked right through it?

Impossible.

But maybe not.

In any case, it was too dangerous. No, she needed a different approach.

So early the next morning, before the sun was even up, she made another frantic search for Danny. When she couldn't find him, she moved quickly to plan B. Like her mother, she was a woman of action, and she felt the need to *do* something.

She went to her room and dug through books until she found another equation, this one about the behavior of magnets. She and Danny were like magnets, she thought. They were opposites in a way. They were also similar. So, she thought, she would see if she could manipulate their magnetic properties simply by giving Danny this formula.

In the back of her mind, she also hoped that maybe just having the formula on a piece of paper would bring him back to her. Maybe he wouldn't be able to resist the pull.

And if he did come back to her, what then? Might the formula also work the opposite way and repel them?

It was a calculated risk that could affect their relationship, but the odds seemed in her favor. No, she reasoned with herself, it was harmless enough. And she could directly observe the outcome. It was perfect.

8

Bridget flung open Danny's door at eight-thirty the next morning. "Where have you been?" she said. "I was up most of the night thinking about what happened yesterday and I've been looking all over for you."

"Don't you knock?" he said, rubbing his eyes. "What time is it?"

Bridget had the same expression she wore whenever he found her wandering in a field with her nose in a book, that look that seemed surprised to find that the world actually existed. Time was like that for her, too. Something other people worried about. It meant almost nothing to Bridget.

"I don't know," she mumbled, looking around for a clock. "Nine or something. How should I know?"

"Because you're *awake*."

"Didn't I tell you?"

He sat up and rubbed his eyes. "You were up most of the night."

She smiled. "I did tell you. I knew I had." Then she hopped onto his bed, pushed her glasses up on her nose, and stared at him. Her look was stern, as if she were about to discipline him. "And," she said, "I was looking for you. Where were you? I looked everywhere. I searched the house, the barn, the fields. I almost went by Sarah Evans's house."

"Very funny."

"Where were you?"

"Right here."

"Oh, no you weren't. I looked here every ten minutes. You definitely were *not* here."

Danny shrugged. He wasn't ready to tell her where he'd been or what had happened. He wasn't even sure he knew himself what had happened in the barn. She said she'd been there, but he hadn't seen her, and it seemed she hadn't seen him, either.

She pretended not to notice his silence. "So I came by to see if you wanted to help me," she said.

He looked at her sideways. "Help you as in help you find some clean socks, or help you as in do something dangerous that you're too smart to do yourself?"

"It isn't *very* dangerous."

"That's what I thought," he said. "How about I find you some clean socks?"

She smiled. "You know I don't usually wear socks," she said. "And anyway, this is important."

Danny rolled his eyes and Bridget waited. He would give in. He always did.

"What is it?"

She pulled another sheet of paper from her pocket, unfolded it, and handed it to him. "Just carry this around."

"I'm still carrying this other one."

"Is it working?"

"I don't know. What's it supposed to do?"

"Now you want to know?"

He nodded. "I think it's time."

"Okay. It's Einstein's general theory of relativity. It's about space-time."

"What?"

"It's hard to explain." She studied him. "Did you *go* anywhere last night?"

"What do you mean *go*?"

"You know . . . *travel*."

He gave her that suspicious look reserved for the suddenly insane. "No."

"Just checking."

"So maybe it doesn't work after all," he said. "Maybe your theory is wrong." He tried to make his voice as dismissive as possible. He didn't like the way Bridget was staring at him.

"Maybe." She watched him. "But just in case, I want to try something else," she announced.

Danny was staring out the window above his desk. It looked like a nice day, the kind of day that might surprise you, if you got lucky. But he wanted a *pleasant* surprise and he wasn't sure that that was what Bridget had in mind.

He looked at her sideways again. "What do you want to try?"

"Just take it."

She held the paper out to him and shook it a few times. He sighed, wondering what might come from *this* piece of paper. A father in Boston with a jet and passports for the two of them to go to the Galápagos Islands? A father with a catamaran, eager to sail him off to Saint Kitts or Nevis? A father who had these things *and* knew who Bridget was? *It's all possible, isn't it?* he thought.

A father. Always a father. Why did he never dream of his mother? Why was she always . . . *gone?*

The word sprang into his mind the instant he touched the paper, and that déjà vu feeling made his spine tingle. He shivered as he and Bridget held the paper between them. Then she let go, and just as she did, they heard their father calling to them from the foot of the stairs. He was announcing a family meeting.

Bridget looked at Danny, at his fingers where they touched the paper. He panicked and quickly opened his hand, and they watched the paper float to the floor between them.

"Too late," she said, studying him carefully.

"Coincidence," he said.

"Maybe." She watched him pick up the paper, fold it, and put it in his back pocket.

"Here we go," he muttered. His face looked drawn and sad.

"You don't have to," she said. "You know, carry it around."

"It's okay," he said.

"And you certainly don't have to carry around both. I'll take that other one."

"No," he said, "I'll keep that one, too."

"Why?"

"Just in case." But he didn't explain further. Then he turned to her. His eyes looked anxious. "Maybe it's not a bad meeting," he said.

Bridget gave him that ever-patient stare, the kind that looked like she could wait a lifetime if it took that long for Danny to think about what he was saying.

"Try to remember," he said to her, "that even though you're a genius, you're still only *twelve*. It's not like you know *everything*."

She pointed to his back pocket. "I guess we'll see, won't we?"

He felt himself grow defensive. "It might not be bad. You don't know."

She was halfway down the stairs, but she stopped again. "Let's review, shall we?" she said.

Shall we? Danny rolled his eyes. He hated the librarian voice. Especially when it came from a seventh grader.

"Family meeting number one," she continued, "Dad announces that we have to put Jasper to sleep so he won't get run over by the van again. Family meeting number two, Dad tells us that Grampa Joe has cancer. Number three, he tells us Grampa Joe is dead. Number four, the TV is blown to pieces and we can't afford a new one. Number five, we have an unexplainable rodent and insect problem that certain people get *blamed* for, and it costs so much to get rid of that we have to cancel our summer vacation. This is family meeting number six. See a pattern?"

He didn't answer.

"The question," she said, "is what will it be about? Lost employment? Broken car? Foreclosure?" She stared at Danny and smiled. "Getting any ideas from your pocket?"

"No," he lied. "And for your information, we already own the house."

"Ever heard of a tax lien? A second mortgage?"

"No."

"You don't pay much attention to what's going on around here, do you?"

"Like you're any better."

"True. Except I'm a girl and that probably helps." She looked at him carefully out of the corner of her eye. "That pocket okay?"

"Fine," he said.

"Nothing strange going on?"

"Nope," he lied. "Let's go."

The truth was that it felt as if someone had built a small bonfire in his pocket, and it was starting to hurt. He had stopped on the stairs to see if it would calm down. Every time he moved his leg, it felt as if something was searing into his backside. He turned his head and sniffed over his shoulder for a hint of smoke in the air.

"What are you doing?"

"Nothing," he said. "I'm coming. Sorry."

The piece of paper continued to throb in his pocket. By

the time they reached the living room he was positive that there had to be a charred hole in the seat of his shorts.

They all took their places in the living room. It wasn't as if they were assigned seats. They each just sat where they always sat. Simon took his place on the couch beside their mother. He was biting on a hangnail, but he nodded to Danny and Bridget when they came into the room, and then shook his head and smiled as if to say, "Here we go again."

Their father sat hunched in the wingback. Bridget and Danny sat on the floor beside the coffee table.

As soon as Danny sat down, the burning in his pocket got more intense, and all he could think about was his father in the barn. And there he was, in the photograph on the bookshelf beside Simon. His father and Jerome in the Himalayas. Danny had a vague recollection that there was a story behind the photo—something about an accident— that his father didn't like to talk about. Probably had something to do with the Free Tibet Society penance, Danny guessed. His father looked so different. It was his father, that was clear, but it wasn't the Cuke, really. No, it was a photo of his other father. How strange to see them both together like this: on one side of the room sat the Cuke, and on the other side of the room, this photo of a man who seemed to be the same man who waited for him in the barn, holding a whip that he wanted to give to Danny. What was happening?

Danny shifted so he wasn't sitting on the pocket of fire, and he caught Bridget's eye. "Look," she whispered, nodding toward their father. "Note cards again."

"What did you expect?" Danny said.

The three children knew that the meetings were their mother's idea. She set the agenda, organized the talking points, and scripted the event. She probably should have led the meetings herself, but she had a strange need for her husband to do it. It was a job for the head of the household, she believed. And she also believed—or hoped, anyway—that if she put her husband in that position, if she made him a successful head of the household by showing him how to do it—setting up meetings, writing agendas, showing him the way—then he would one day *become* the head of the household. She wished for it. Longed for it.

But it never happened.

And at this meeting, it was worse than ever. Wade Parsons, his eyes red and watery, sat hunched over the small pile of note cards in his hands. He shuffled through them one after the other, stopping now and again to read one, scratch his head, squint at the handwriting. The script was blocky, bold capital letters penned with a Magic Marker. It was Claire's handwriting. She had written, organized, and numbered them.

And his father was going to read them. The way he always did.

He cleared his throat a few times, wiped his eyes, scratched his bald head, organized the cards one more time, double-checking the numbers to be sure they were in the correct order. He took a sip of water from a glass beside him. And everyone waited.

But sitting on the floor, Danny was in agony.

"What's in my pocket?" he whispered to Bridget.

"Why? Is something happening?"

"Just tell me," he hissed.

"It's a formula for magnetic properties."

"Like how magnets stick together?"

"Sort of," she said. "It's about how they attract *and* repel each other. The same equation works for both." He was silent, and she whispered to him with more concern than he had ever heard in her voice before. "Why, Danny? What's happening?"

He looked straight ahead and didn't answer for a moment. "You probably should have given me one that's just for attraction." She stared at him, her eyes wide and questioning. But he didn't know what to say to her. He didn't know the answer to the question she was asking him with her eyes. "I just have a bad feeling," he said.

And then, as if they'd all been given a secret signal, everyone turned to where their father sat. They could hear the scratch of his nails against his scalp, the rub of his fingers against the cards as he flipped them. Danny held his breath. He focused on the laces of Simon's shoes, which he could see under the coffee table. He didn't mean to fall into a dream—didn't wish it. He was trying to keep his head, keep his mind off the burning in his pocket, when suddenly *he is the second son of a great German psychiatrist and he possesses powers that would shock the world. Special agents of the government, fearing these powers, kidnap him and place him in the home of an unsuspecting and entirely mediocre family in northern New England, where he lives happily, normally, until one day his extraordinary gifts begin to show themselves. He suddenly can—*

"Ouch," he said.

Everyone in the room was staring at him. He glared at Bridget and rubbed his side, where she'd obviously pinched him. But she looked at him with the most appalling mask of innocence, and he knew he'd never be able to prove it. "Sorry," he said to the room. "I had a muscle cramp."

Simon smiled as if it were one of the funniest things he'd seen in a long time, then shook his head in the way that says "What a moron."

At last his father cleared his throat, and everyone turned away from Danny and faced his father. He began to read from his cards.

"Let's see," he mumbled, his voice halting and unsteady. "We've called you together to let you know about some changes that are going to be taking place in the family. They're very"—he paused and squinted at the card—"*exciting* changes. I know you'll be excited by them." He looked up and smiled wearily so that his smile matched his voice. The gesture and the words were meant to look and sound hopeful, but they just weren't. They were sad.

Danny glanced around the room. Not a single face returned his father's smile. Every face looked just like his father's. They were looking for hope, but they weren't finding it. And the word *excited* hung in the air like a bad joke.

"Your mother has been given a very rare opportunity

to return to school and finish her graduate degree in physics. She got the letter"—he turned to her—"the day before yesterday?"

"That's right," she said, turning to her children. She smiled, too, her face almost longing for hope.

"Wow, Mom," Bridget said. "That's great."

"It is." Their mother beamed.

Their father cleared his throat. "She starts in mid-August."

"That soon?" Simon said. "I thought the semester didn't start until mid-September."

"Registration and committee meetings," their mother explained.

"So," their father continued, "for convenience and so your mother can concentrate on her studies, we've decided that it would be"—he paused again—"*best* if she took an apartment close to the campus."

"Why?" Simon asked. "The school is only a few miles from here. Wouldn't it be cheaper to just get another car?"

"I can get loan money for an apartment," she explained, "but not for a car."

"You're moving out because you can get loan money?" Simon asked.

"You're moving out?" Bridget said. "What do you mean you're moving out?"

"Everyone calm down," their father said. "It's okay. We've talked about this and worked it out. This is the best solution."

"Best for who?" Simon asked. "Mom? You?"

"Best for everyone," their mother said.

The burning in Danny's pocket suddenly grew more intense than he thought he could bear. And that was when it occurred to him: his parents, like magnets, were separating.

He turned to Bridget. His first reaction was that this was her fault. She'd given him the formula. He was just a— what did Bridget call it? That thing that helps things happen but isn't really part of it?—a catalyst, that was it. He was just a catalyst. This was all Bridget's fault. *She* chose the equations. *She* wrote them down. *She* was the experimenter. He was just a catalyst. He just carried them.

He looked at his father reading cards that his mother had written. His father, like him, was just the catalyst. And that made them the same. Again.

He stared at Bridget out of the corner of his eye as hard as he could without looking too obvious. He wanted her to know that he knew what she was doing to him. But she continued to look at their father.

"I can't believe this is happening," Simon mumbled from the couch. He glared at his father. Then he turned and spoke to his mother. "I can't believe you're *doing* this."

Their mother spoke again, her voice hard. "It's for the *best*. Your father and I agree."

"Don't lie to us. *He* didn't decide this. *You* did. This isn't an idea *he* could have come up with," Simon said, sneering.

"That's enough, young man. Your father and I talked—"

"You mean *you* talked."

"I mean *we* talked. And this is what *we* decided."

Simon turned to his father. "Is that true, Dad? Did you decide this, too?"

His father rubbed his head and flipped a card. He looked at Simon briefly. "This is a complicated situation, Simon," he said. Then he turned back to the cards in his hand. "Your mother and I only want what's best for you."

Simon almost laughed. "Is that what it says there, Dad? Is that what she told you to say?"

"That's enough," his mother said.

"That's what I thought," Simon said. "But I get it. This is what it means to be the water, isn't it?"

His father looked up at him but didn't speak.

"Be the water. Tend your garden where it blooms. I've been listening to you mouth this same crap since I was *born,* and it means *nothing.* It's a lie like all of this is a lie. And you're living it. You both are."

"Simon," his mother said, reaching for his arm. Her voice was pleading, wishful.

He recoiled quickly as if she were trying to rub a dead fish on his arm. "Don't touch me."

"We've worked it out so there will be very little disruption to the family," their father said. He rubbed his head, then looked down at his cards and said, "Your lives will basically be exactly the same."

"Shut up!" Simon shouted. Then he stood and said to his mother, "Tell him to shut up. He always does what you tell him to do," he added, turning back to his father, "unless you tell him to be a *man.*"

Then he walked out of the room.

As he passed, their father lifted his eyes, but Simon, without looking at him, swung his hand at the cards his father was holding and scattered them all over the floor.

"Simon!" their mother said. But he was already gone.

She turned and looked at her husband for what seemed like the first time. "I think we're done, Wade."

He stared at her and hesitated. Then he gathered the cards from the floor and put them in his pocket.

Their mother pursed her lips and shook her head. Then she stood. "Well, that didn't go like I'd hoped." Her voice caught in her throat and she put her fingers to her mouth. "No," she said to her husband, "don't get up."

"Mom?" Danny said. "What is it?"

She laughed and lifted her eyes to the ceiling, wiping the tears from them before they stained her cheeks. Then she turned to Danny and tried to smile. "It's not quite working out like I'd planned," she said. "Not at all like I'd planned. But then your father knows what I'm talking about."

"You're really moving out?" Bridget asked.

She nodded. "I think I have to."

"Why?"

"Because no one has asked me to stay."

"I want you to stay," Bridget said.

She smiled. "I know, sweetheart. And I wish that were enough."

"Why isn't it?" Bridget said. "We *all* want you to stay. I know we do."

Danny looked up and tried to smile, but his pocket *really* hurt and it came out looking more like a grimace. His father stared at his shoes.

"I'm sure you do," their mother said.

Then, from the corner, their father spoke. "What did

you want me to do? How was I supposed to *fight* you on this?"

"Do you think I wanted a *fight,* Wade? I didn't want a fight."

"What, then?"

"You don't get it, do you?" She laughed under her breath again and closed her eyes. "When I met you, you were so full of hope and life. You were a mess, but in a dreamy sort of way that looked like it was going some-where. And I wanted to walk with you—go with you on that journey. But something happened. You stopped. And with you, all the hope and life that I fell in love with. It's like you lost yourself. And for a dozen years you've been walking around lost."

He stared at his cards. Danny looked quickly at Bridget, but she was frozen, watching.

"Even now you're lost, aren't you?" Their mother laughed quietly through her nose. "You were right the other day, about doors closing. You were prepared to walk through a door, but it closed before you could go through it, and your whole life you've been standing in front of that door, wishing it would open again. But it won't. And the sad part is that, because you keep staring at that closed door, you don't see the other doors in your life that are wide open. That's why you feel lost. That's why you feel trapped. Because you've trapped yourself."

She turned to Bridget and Danny. "But I can't be trapped, too," she said.

For some strange reason, the formula in his pocket

gave Danny hope. Maybe this was happening just because of math and science. Maybe it was just about magnetism, something *physical,* not circumstantial, not personal. And if that was the case, then Bridget could just write a new formula that would make everything right again.

Better yet, Bridget could write a formula that would turn the Wade Parsons in front of him, the one wearing the SuperValu uniform and reading from cards, into the Wade Parsons in the barn with a whip. If it was just about science and math, then wasn't it possible that the man in front of him might be able to become that other man, to become the man who stood in the picture on the bookshelf?

"Dad?" he said, his voice small in the room. "Is there anything that could change your mind?" He looked at his father but, getting no response, turned to his mother. "Is there?"

For the second time in the meeting, his mother looked at him. Sometimes when she did that, her eyes got that far-away look, and it was as if she weren't looking at Danny at all but at something else, as if she were staring into a dream that *almost* came true. When she blinked, it was gone. "That's really up to your father, Danny."

The entire room turned to Wade Parsons and waited. He rubbed his head until it was polished to a shine. The whole room watched, barely breathing, as if they'd all just offered him something. They were his, they seemed to be saying, if he'd just choose them over everything else.

"Wade?" their mother said again, and Danny thought,

Say it, say it. He sat up a little straighter and tried to ignore the burning in his pocket, tried to push the reality of the pain away.

"Dad?" he said.

His father looked at him. It was the first time he'd looked directly at any of them. But just as quickly, his eyes fell back to his lap. "I think this is probably for the best," he said.

"I guess it is," their mother declared. Danny watched as she took a deep breath and stood a little straighter, a little stiffer. She ran her fingers under her eyes one last time, drew her mouth tight across her face, and left the room.

Danny stared at his father. It was happening. What he'd dreamed was coming true—and he'd never been so frightened in his life.

Bridget dug her elbow into Danny's side.

"Ouch," he whispered fiercely. "Will you stop doing that?"

"It's happening, Danny. You're making it happen."

His worst fears, spoken out loud by a seventh grader. He tried not to listen. "Thanks to you," he snapped.

"But *you're* making it happen."

Danny turned to her with a look of confusion and fury. Why had she given him these formulas if she'd thought this might happen? What was she *thinking*? "In case you forgot," he hissed, "I'm not doing it by myself. You're picking the formulas. And you're not doing a very good job of it."

She stared back at him. Then she nodded.

He turned to his father. "Are we done?" Danny asked, rising quickly.

His father looked at him again, his eyes wide, as if he were surprised to see Danny there—surprised to see either of them there. "Yes, I think so," he said. "Yes, we're done."

"Good." And Danny was gone.

9

About an hour after the family meeting, Danny stood in the doorway of Bridget's room and watched her. She was hunched over her small desk, her thin shoulders draped in a T-shirt. Large open textbooks were piled around her and she flipped through one quickly, writing things in her notebook, adjusting her glasses, writing some more. She worked with an energy Danny could never seem to give to studying. She worked like she didn't know how to do anything else, like the work was a part of her.

Danny knocked softly.

Bridget turned and, squinting over her glasses, smiled at him. "Hey," she said so softly that it almost sounded like an apology.

"B, what's going on?"

She pushed her glasses up and, still looking at the papers in front of her, waved him into the room. Danny paused for a second, watching her a bit longer, and thought that sometimes she seemed so old. It was as if she'd never been a child, as if she'd been born an adult and couldn't understand why the rest of the world never saw her that way.

A pair of shorts and a winter hat covered the place on her bed that he'd cleared the day before, but they were easy to move. He sat down and watched her cross her legs just the way he'd seen their mother do a thousand times. "I don't know what's going on," she said. "Something happened in the shed when you touched those formulas. It's like you've opened up the potential of the quantum world, just by *touching* symbols of that potential."

His head swam for a moment, as if he'd just walked into a room full of people who were all asking him questions in a foreign language. "What are you talking about?"

"Sorry," she said. "Let me see if I can explain it better. Do you know about quantum physics? Electrons, protons, stuff like that?"

"Sort of. Sometimes I listen when Mom talks with you about her work. I'm not really sure, but I think it's something about really small things and everything is made of them."

"Close enough. Every molecule is made up of these incredibly tiny particles that spin around each other. We can't see them, but we know they exist, and scientists have been trying for over a hundred years to understand more about them."

"What's to understand? Little stuff makes big stuff."

"It isn't that simple, Einstein."

"Why not?"

She pushed her glasses up on her face. "Because the quantum world is—I don't know—different, and it's not just that it's really small. It's different in ways that it shouldn't be different. It's different in ways that almost completely reverse the way we normally think about science.

"Don't look at me like that," she continued. "Here, I'll give you a really good example." She tore a piece of paper from her notebook. He couldn't help noticing the picture of Barbie on the cover. "A present for my eighth birthday," she explained. "From Grampa Joe, of course."

"Back when he was trying to make you into a girl?" Danny asked, smiling.

She screwed up her face in disgust without looking up from the paper, where she was jotting down some notes. "I don't know if you've noticed," she began, "but scientists are actually very logical people. We like cause and effect. We know that water freezes at a temperature below thirty-two degrees Fahrenheit, so when we put water in a freezer set at below thirty-two degrees, the water will freeze. Most science is like that."

"You mean, most science is *boring* like that?"

"I mean *predictable* and *logical*. And because the world is predictable and logical, you'd assume that the quantum world would be, wouldn't you? Because logical things have to come from logical things. Right?"

"I guess. But what just happened didn't feel particularly logical. It felt a little weird and unpredictable, if you ask me."

"Exactly. That's what got me thinking about quantum

physics. See, the quantum world isn't predictable or logical at all. And that's why it's so mysterious to scientists. It turns out that the quantum world is actually completely unpredictable and appears to be absolutely random."

"Sounds like the quantum world is a lot like people."

"I hadn't thought of that." She stared at him. "Are you okay?"

"I guess. I mean, our whole family is falling apart, and that isn't helping."

"No."

"But, Bridget, what if it isn't science? What if it's . . . I don't know . . . what if it's just *me*? What if I'm making it happen and it has nothing to do with science at all?"

She studied him. "Do you know something you aren't telling me?"

"No," he lied. "I was just, you know, wondering."

She smiled. "Occam's razor," she said. "Let's not assume more than we need to. Science looks like the only assumption we can reasonably make—if there's anything reasonable about any of this. Let's keep it simple."

"Do you think we can fix it?"

"I think so. Hang in there for a minute more and let me teach you some science. Then we can figure out what to do next."

"Okay," he said. "So, the quantum world is unpredictable and random."

"Exactly."

"But that means that in the quantum world, *anything* could happen."

She nodded. "Doesn't it look like anything *is* happening?

103

Who could have predicted this? It has to be something at the quantum level."

"How do you know it isn't just crazy human behavior?"

"Because if it is," she said, "then we can't do anything about it. It makes me feel better believing we can fix something we broke." Her eyes met his. "The problem is that if we're right, it looks like you're the key. That's what I meant earlier. You've—I don't know—*opened* something."

"I don't understand. Why me?"

"I'm not sure yet, but I think it has to do with a theory called the uncertainty principle." She shot him a quick glance as she grabbed her pencil again. "Don't panic. I'll draw you a picture."

She drew quickly and then turned the paper toward him so he could see it. In the center she'd drawn a circle with a bunch of wavy lines inside it.

"You know how if you take a high-speed photo of a baseball pitch, you can say, 'Right here, as the ball left the pitcher's hand, it was traveling eighty-six miles per hour'? You say, 'The ball is here, traveling at this speed'?"

"Yeah."

"Well, in the quantum world you can't do that. And that's the uncertainty principle. You can never say where an electron is *and* how fast it's going. Never."

"Why not?"

"I'll show you. Look here." They stood over the paper. Bridget pushed a tangle of hair behind her ear. It was such a grown-up gesture that Danny had to remind himself again that she was just a girl. She was his *little* sister. She was the sister *he has been sent to protect from a Serbian splinter group intent on uncovering deep scientific secrets to sell on the black market—*

"Ouch!" he cried.

"Are you paying attention?"

He held his ribs where she'd poked him. "That really hurt."

"You were doing it again."

"I think it's a subconscious reaction to stress," he said. He looked at the room and the desk and tried to reconnect with something. "What are we talking about?"

"The uncertainty principle?"

"Right."

She shook her head. "Just look at the picture."

"What is it?"

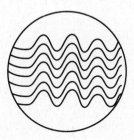

She smiled. "This is a picture of a simple electron in a bucket."

"Is it underwater?"

"No. There isn't any water in the bucket. Just an electron."

"Then what's with all the waves?"

"That's the electron."

He shook his head to clear it. As often happened in conversations with Bridget, he understood every word she said, but when he put them together, they didn't make any sense. "I don't get it."

She pushed her glasses up. "*That's* the problem. This is what it looks like when we measure the *speed* of the electron in the bucket. Electrons move just like waves, so we have to measure them like waves. But if you wanted to see where the electron *is,* then we'd have to measure it as a particle"—she drew a circle with a dot off to one side of it—"and say, 'Here it is.' But when we do that, the waves—the speed—disappear. We can't know both things because we can't measure an electron as a wave *and* as a particle."

"But which one is it? Is an electron a wave or a particle?"

She smiled. "It's *both.* And it appears to behave however it wants. Going where it wants, changing however it wants."

"So what does this have to do with me?"

She'd begun doodling on the page: swirling lines that coiled and uncoiled, stretched and then gathered themselves along the edge of the paper. "It sounds weird, but I think you're able to get inside the uncertainty principle. You're able to see the quantum world as both particle and wave. When you hold those formulas, you somehow open the potential of the world so that it becomes something it wasn't meant to be. You touch chaos theory and it becomes possible, even though technically—*logically*—it isn't supposed to. You hold on to the general theory of relativity and . . ." She stared at him. "Nothing happened then, did it?"

"I don't think so."

"It seemed like you just disappeared. Did you go anywhere? Move into a different place in space-time?"

"I don't even know what you're talking about."

"Hmmm," she said, continuing to stare at Danny in a way that made him very uncomfortable. "That's the only anomaly in the pattern," she continued. "Everything else behaves according to the theory. Chaos theory, magnetic forces. In those instances, you touched the papers and the theories became real, but in the ways of quantum mechanics. Just as an electron can't be measured as a wave *and* a particle, in the same way magnetic theory can't influence human behavior. But with you, both things seem to be happening."

"But why me?"

"I don't know yet," she said. "But we have to find out. And there's something missing. Something has already happened to make this situation even *possible,* and I don't know what it is." She looked at him hard. "That first formula I gave you, are you *sure* nothing weird happened to you when you carried it around?"

You mean, did I meet my father in the barn—the father I'm supposed to have—and did he have a huge whip but absolutely no idea who you are? Not a good time to drop that bomb.

"Positive," he lied.

"Very strange," she said, still staring at him.

"I don't know, Bridget," he said, trying to deflect attention, "this sounds crazy."

"Crazier than the other stuff I just told you?" she said,

turning back to her desk. "Crazier than the idea that this pencil, that hat you threw on the floor—which is my favorite hat, by the way—that everything in this room is made up of little tiny particles that do what they want and can't be talked about in any reasonable way?"

No. It was true. This science was weird. Even if you didn't care about science, you had to admit that it was pretty bizarre. And he had proof—more proof than he was willing to share with Bridget.

10

How do parents go on with their lives after a conversation like the one they've just had?

Danny sat in his room and listened to the sounds in the house, trying to determine whether there was any movement. But the house was silent. He smelled the air. Nothing. Not even dinner.

He crept down to the first floor and listened again. Still nothing. In the living room he stopped in front of the photograph of his father and Jerome in Tibet. Just yesterday he had seen this same man in the barn. Danny didn't know how that had happened or why, but he found himself longing for that feeling again—to hold a whip, to live up to someone's expectations, to *do* something. Was it even real? Or was it some strange dream that *felt* real? He wasn't sure.

"Your father used to be quite adventurous." His mother was right behind him.

"You scared me," he said.

"I'm sorry." She smiled, but, as earlier, it was a sad smile.

Danny turned back to the photograph. "What happened to him?"

"What happens to most people, I guess," she said. "They grow up, their priorities change, and they realize that other parts of them are more important."

"Can't you have both?"

"Both what?" she asked.

"The adventurous side and the other side—you know, the *boring* side."

She ran her fingers through his hair and smiled sadly. "You can't have anything you don't make room for, no matter what it is. And sometimes it's easier to say, 'I'll do that again later.' "

"Is that what Dad said?"

"Years ago? Probably. But now—oh, Danny," and she reached up and again ran her fingers through his hair, the same hair his father had once had. "I don't know what happened. Except that your father does feel lost."

Danny felt her hand drop from his head, and then she turned to go. "Mom?" he said. She looked at him and at the photo and understood the question he wanted to ask but couldn't.

"I'd take the man in that photo back if he showed up," she said. "I'd take him back in a second."

Then she was gone. She walked with stiff determination. She looked like a woman who had moved on.

Danny felt an uncomfortable heat coming from his pocket.

From the kitchen his mother shouted, "Oh my goodness! Wade! Wade, come down here. I have to show you something."

Danny heard the sound of feet rushing down the stairs, and by the time he walked into the kitchen, Bridget and his father were already there. The hope of good news drew them like a cool breeze on a hot day. Simon hadn't been seen again since the family meeting.

"The mail came," their mother said, waving a letter in the air. "Come here, everyone. And listen. This is extremely important."

Danny looked quickly at Bridget, but she was looking at her mother. His father was looking at his hands.

Their mother smoothed out the letter and cleared her throat. "This arrived for Bridget just today. It's so exciting. Listen to this. 'Dear Bridget,' " she read, turning to Bridget and smiling, " 'it is with great pleasure that we extend to you an invitation to join the Youth Scholarship Academy for the upcoming academic year. We are very impressed with your application and view your enrollment as a wonderful addition to an already exciting program.

" 'As a student of the academy,' " she continued, " 'you will have an opportunity to immerse yourself in some of the most advanced ideas and experiments in quantum physics, molecular biology, and advanced mathematics' "—she looked up and gave Bridget another big smile—

" 'and you will be working with others equally talented and interested in these pursuits. To enroll . . .' Blah, blah, blah. Here's how it ends: 'Please know that you are one of the most academically talented students we have ever enrolled in the academy—you are certainly the youngest—and we look forward with great eagerness to your joining the academy for the upcoming semester. Sincerely, Mark Campbell, Dean of Admissions, College of Science and Technology.'

"Can you believe it?" their mother said. "She got in, Wade. She got in! Bridget, you got in!" She leaned over and hugged her daughter so hard that Danny thought Bridget's eyes would pop.

"Congratulations, sweetheart," their father said. He smiled. It *was* good news, almost good enough to bring some joy into their lives.

Then why, thought Danny, *is my pocket on fire?*

"I didn't know I had applied," Bridget said.

Their mother waved her hand in dismissal and turned to the letter again. "Oh, B, we didn't want to get your hopes up too high and then have you be disappointed. Your dad and I just thought this might be a great opportunity for you. And now you'll have your chance."

"But I won't be going to my school?"

"No, dear. You'll get to go to the college, where you can actually *learn* something."

"Oh." Bridget turned to Danny. He'd never seen her look so panicked. Never.

"Don't you have something to say to your sister?" their mother said, turning to Danny.

"Nice going, B," Danny said.

But Danny didn't think about the academy; he didn't think about how great this was for Bridget. He thought about how, in her room, he'd had that thought of Bridget being a scientist he'd been sent to protect from Serbian terrorists intent on kidnapping her. And he felt, strangely, as if he'd *failed*. He'd done it again. He'd had a dream and made it come true. And now every good feeling that he'd brought with him into the kitchen had just been blown to smithereens.

His pocket! He put his hand on it, and fear struck him so hard in the chest that he could barely breathe.

"And really, Wade," their mother said, "now that I think about it, it makes perfect sense for Bridget to live with me, closer to the college. Otherwise, I don't see how you could get her there every day *and* get the boys off at a reasonable hour. Don't you agree?"

"Bridget live with you?" he asked.

"Yes. It's the only logical solution, really. She and I could walk to school together, maybe take some classes together. We'll be like roommates," she said to Bridget, smiling.

Danny stared at her. Her face almost glowed. He'd seen that look before. It was the look she had had just after the shed exploded. It was the look she'd had when she held up the prisms. It was the look he'd seen her give her husband only once in the past few years: when he opened that letter and read it to them. But the look hadn't lasted. It was like a flash of color from a swinging prism, and Danny suddenly felt as if they were living a prism life—each of them an individual color, separated and dividing.

"Well, I don't know, Claire. That's a pretty big decision."

She squared her shoulders to him. "It seems no bigger than the other decisions we've been making so quickly this week," she said.

He looked at his hands, then pushed them into his pockets. "Still, it seems worth having a discussion."

"Why?"

"I just don't think that we should make a decision like this because of issues of transportation," he said. "We will have Simon driving, you know."

"Yes, but you'll only have one car," she reminded him. "And Simon's insurance is still a question mark."

Their father paused. "I'd still like to talk about it a bit more."

She sighed. "I'm happy to talk about it, Wade, if you think we'll actually arrive at a different conclusion. Is that what you want? Do you want us to arrive at a different conclusion so Bridget can stay with you, even though it will make your life much more difficult?"

He scratched at his elbow. "I just want to be part of the process."

"Fine. Why don't you begin by listing the benefits of having Bridget stay here with you?"

"I would have my room," Bridget said.

"This is a discussion I'm having with your father, sweetie," her mother said.

"In front of all of us," Bridget said.

"Nevertheless." Their mother turned to her husband. "Wade?"

"It just feels a little hasty," he said.

She sighed. "It is," she said, her voice quiet and sad. "It's very hasty. And I know how much that must upset you, I really do. But we have to think of Bridget, Wade. She needs to come first in this."

"Then don't I get a say?" Bridget asked.

Her mother turned to her. "Not this time, sweetie. This is a decision your father and I need to make."

"Why?"

"Because we're the grown-ups."

They all turned to their father and watched as he rubbed his head, scratched his elbow some more, and crammed his hands into his pockets again. "Well," he finally said, "if you think so, I guess it does make a lot of sense." He pulled his hands out of his pockets and stared at them again. "All right then," he said.

Danny stared at his parents in disbelief. His mother pored over the letter again and again with pride, and his father busied himself at the sink, brooding over pans that were already clean and wiping spotless countertops—anything to keep his hands busy.

Bridget leaned over and whispered into Danny's ear, "Come to my room *now*."

"I have to do something first," he said. He didn't understand why, but something told him he needed to go to the barn. He needed to touch that whip, to know if the life he'd seen just twenty-four hours ago was still possible.

Because right now *anything* seemed better than this life he was living.

"Are you kidding? What could be more important than . . . *this*?" she asked.

"*Something.* I'll come by later."

Bridget would work out answers her way, but he needed to work out answers *his* way.

He headed for the barn.

11

Bridget sat at her desk and stared. Her palms lay flat on her desk on either side of a blank sheet of paper, a stub of pencil just out of reach of her right ring finger. On the outside she was all calm and serenity.

But inside she was fighting conflicting emotions.

On the one hand was the thrill of discovery. She was approaching something she'd almost never had the nerve to *dream* of, and yet here she was. Each equation she gave to Danny filled her with a thrill she'd never felt before. It was exciting, intoxicating. It made her feel like the most powerful person in the world. To imagine something was to make it real. The mysteries were there before her, on the other side of an unlocked door, and she needed only to open it and keep writing.

On the other hand, there was Danny. And her family. It was very likely that *she* was responsible for the breakup of the family. All these lives thrown into turmoil for an experiment. She pursued knowledge, consequences be damned.

But there was also this sinking understanding that got clearer and clearer every day. She'd seen Danny staring at the photograph of her father and his friend Jerome in the Himalayas, but whenever she looked at the picture, her father didn't look at all familiar to her. She'd never known him as that adventurous, confident man. She'd only known him as he was now. And she'd come to understand that that transformation had to have taken place right around the time *she* was born. So she was responsible for it on that level, too.

And then she thought about Danny: Danny who took those pieces of paper, Danny who seemed to just walk into trouble, Danny who looked more and more like their father, Danny who never stopped trusting her.

It was the trusting that made her feel the most responsible. Because the truth was, Bridget wasn't entirely sure what she was doing. The formulas made sense, but in Danny's hands they had power—real power that frightened Bridget even as it thrilled her.

That afternoon, when Danny stopped by her room, she decided to end it.

"We're done," she said.

"I don't think so," he said.

"It's too dangerous."

"But we *did* this, B. We can't stop now."

She looked at the floor. "I don't know if I can fix it."

"What choice do we have? You have to keep trying."

"Fine."

"And in the meantime, I'm keeping these formulas with me."

"Why?" she asked.

"Because at least we *know* what they do. With these, things feel predictable. You have to figure out how to *reverse* them."

"Are you sure you want to keep doing this, Danny?" she asked.

"I'm sure."

"Okay," she muttered. "If you're sure."

"I am," he said, but he didn't look sure. He looked afraid.

Bridget was afraid of something, too. And she knew she was right to fear it.

Because the moment Danny left her room with those formulas in his pocket, things started to change for her.

Her room, for one. Several times that afternoon, and for many days that followed, she walked into her room to find that it was different. It was her room on the surface, except that something *beneath* the surface was changing. There were times when nothing in her room felt solid, there and not there at the same time. She could see her room—the unmade bed, the littered floor, wrappers and plates and cups here and there—but if she looked at it sideways, in that half-blurred view out of the corner of her eye, she could almost perceive another room *underneath* her room—as if her room were superimposed over a room that was *not* her room. She called it the underroom.

There were no clothes on the floor in the underroom, and the bed was always made. There were framed water-color landscapes on the wall and lace curtains on the windows. It looked like a guest room, and it was painted a light green. Bridget didn't understand what it meant. Why had her experiments with the quantum order of things brought forth a room that was not her room at all? She didn't know.

A few days later, the feeling got stronger and began to affect everything, not just her room. At the lunch counter in the kitchen, she could see a family underneath her family. They were basically the same, looked the same, acted the same. But they moved around her—even *through* her—as if she weren't there. Seeing that other world was like looking at her life through tracing paper. She called that place the underuniverse. And she didn't tell anyone about it.

What would she say? "I made a mess and now I'm paying for it, too"? What does a person say in this situation? "Help"? Who could help her? Only she could. If she had enough time.

12

During the next few weeks, Danny returned again and again to the barn, each time finding his father—or the man who would be his father. They talked about the whip, about power and about the importance of taking chances. They dreamed about the things they would one day do. For the first time ever, Danny didn't have to be the second son of the Cuke. Instead, he could be the second son of a Tibetan whip master—the second son of a world traveler. The son of . . . just of someone else. And being the son of someone else meant that his own destiny opened up before him. He could be anything.

It never struck him as strange that he and his father never left the barn together. For the time being, this life existed only in the barn. To question it was to risk something he didn't dare risk. It often felt as if he was building his new life out of cards, and if he rushed, if he moved too quickly, the whole thing would tumble over. So he took his time. He went to the barn. He waited for his life to happen.

And he never told anyone where he was going or what he was doing.

Not that anybody really cared where he was or what he was doing. The whole family had scattered themselves like so many particles in an explosion. Simon was away from the house most of the time, and although Danny tried to find out where he was, nobody knew for sure. Maybe he had a job. Maybe he was at the gym or the ball field. But when he was home, Simon ate.

Simon had always been a big kid. He'd eat almost anything—cookie crumbs from the table, the crust from someone's sandwich, M&M'S he found jammed in the cushions of the couch. Sometimes he'd get into a food rut and only eat jelly sandwiches for weeks at a time. Dozens of them every day. But over the past week he'd started to get thinner. His cheeks lost that round, jolly look. They were more sunken and hollow and his eyes had gotten really big. Danny would watch him sit at the kitchen counter licking a spatula he'd buried in the peanut butter jar until it practically shined, and all the while he was getting thinner and thinner. It was as if the hunger couldn't be satisfied, as if it was devouring Simon, too. It troubled Danny more than he could say.

Danny started keeping a bag of Fig Newtons in the kitchen cupboard and in his room. They were the closest things to a jelly sandwich he could think of. He fed them to Simon whenever he saw him, to keep the hunger at bay.

Then Simon really began to change. He got sullen and angry. He stopped caring about things—even baseball. He was rude and mean to everyone. He never smiled. He became the mean part of himself, but to a higher degree. His meanness, which had been like a flash of light and heat that blinded and burned for a moment, became more intense, more focused, more constant. Simon came to embody meanness. And he meant to hurt.

Danny saw this new Simon one afternoon when he'd gone to the far side of the barn to feed Bunserati. Bunserati was Simon's rabbit. Grampa Joe had given him the rabbit the year before he died, and they'd named him Bunserati because, with his long black ears that lay back on his head, he looked very fast and very Italian, although he wasn't either of those things. Simon loved that rabbit, but after Grampa Joe's death, he'd lost interest in him. That was when Danny and Bridget had taken over his care, which wasn't easy. He was an enormous rabbit, weighing close to twenty-five pounds, and he ate a lot.

Danny brought a cup full of rabbit pellets and a small hunk of lettuce that he'd found in the fridge. He'd just set them in the cage and was running his fingers between Bunserati's ears when Simon suddenly appeared.

"Hello, Dan," he said. *Dan?*

"Want to help?" Danny asked.

"Yeah, right. Like I want to spend my time tending to an animal so fat it would explode if you dropped it."

Danny looked at him sideways but didn't say anything. Who was this person? He looked like Simon, but he didn't act like any Simon Danny had ever seen before.

"I can't believe that stupid old man thought I wanted to have this hopping bag of lard."

"Shut up, Simon," Danny said. "Grampa Joe knew you loved Bunserati."

"Yeah, well, he got *that* one wrong big-time. But he was always a retard."

Danny stood and faced him. How could Simon be talking about Grampa Joe like this? "Why are you saying these things?" Danny asked.

"Because they're *true*," Simon said, emphasizing the last word so strongly that he projected a wad of spit at Danny. "Only another retard would have to ask." Then he stared at Danny, looking him up and down. "But what am I thinking? I'm looking at the *queen* of retards. The grand Pickle, heir to the Cukedom. Poor boy," he said, his voice cracking in a pretend cry.

"Shut up, Simon," Danny said, but Simon didn't hear him. He was laughing out loud as he rounded the barn.

Mean Simon had appeared.

The strange part about it was that Danny would run from Simon's wrath one minute, and in the next minute he'd see him in the kitchen, goofy and friendly and excited about practicing his pitching. When he was like that, Danny gave him every Fig Newton in his pocket. He thought of it as positive reinforcement.

But after a few days Danny came to the conclusion that Fig Newtons didn't really make much of a difference. Simon was either happy or mean and a Fig Newton didn't move him one way or the other. It was weird, almost as if Simon were really two completely different people: Happy Simon and Mean Simon. Danny never saw the two at the same time. If he peeked into Simon's room, Simon was either Happy and invited him in, or he was Mean and threw real darts at Danny's head—a few of which just barely missed. Danny never saw him go from Mean to Happy or Happy to Mean.

He even tested it one morning. He saw Happy Simon in the kitchen with his fingers plunged into a jar of marshmallow Fluff and said, "Hey, Simon, I heard your coach say that if you keep throwing like Dad, you might want to go out for the softball team. He thought that might be your only shot at a college scholarship." It was the meanest thing he could think of.

But Simon just laughed and said, "Softball team. That's funny. Got any Newtons on you?"

Danny learned quickly to recognize the differences between the two Simons so that he could stay out of Mean Simon's way. Telling them apart was pretty simple. They looked almost exactly the same except for one important factor: Mean Simon was a little heavier and he ate nothing. Happy Simon was thin and ate everything. He ate pickles from the jar in the fridge, dipped in mustard and raspberry jelly. He ate frozen florets of broccoli—ice and all. He ate pinto beans right out of the can. He ate huge slices of liverwurst on toast, smothered in horseradish sauce or their father's peach chutney. He ate things people weren't supposed to eat, like the rind of a slice of watermelon and raw cloves of garlic and spoonfuls of barbecue sauce. He ate anything he could find.

He ate as if he were eating for two, and Danny started referring to him as if he *were* two. He called him the Simons.

"Why do you call him that?" Bridget asked.

"Because he eats for two."

"Yeah," she said, "and he's always so happy. Why is that? What is there to be happy about?"

"I don't know," Danny said. He didn't mention Mean Simon. For some reason, Bridget didn't know what he knew, couldn't see what he could see.

Everything seemed to be changing. There were times when Danny felt that the life he had for so long been trying to escape was slowly disappearing on its own. Even Bridget seemed to be more absent than not in the weeks after the family meeting, and there were times when he couldn't find her anywhere for hours. He'd come from the barn eager to talk with her, but she'd be nowhere to be found.

This didn't really surprise him. Things had become so strange that Bridget's behavior seemed as normal as anyone else's. And when he did start to worry, he quickly calmed himself by deciding she was off on a reading hike somewhere. He convinced himself that her habit of pacing while she read must have been getting worse. He imagined her lost in a book several miles from home. Believing that helped him make sense of things when he spent an entire afternoon waiting for her to return.

And now his parents seemed to be there hardly at all. His mother, as his dream had anticipated, was usually gone. She had closed the door on the past and was moving on. She'd signed a lease for a two-bedroom apartment a few blocks from the college. When she was around, that was all she could talk about. The view over the common was too lovely to believe, and, while the bedrooms were a little tight, they'd have plenty of space in the living room for two desks and a sitting area. And there were bookshelves on almost every wall. She called it the girls' pad, like she was eighteen again, which made Danny cringe. She spent the following week at the college, got signed up for classes and "settled in." She hadn't officially moved out, but it felt about as close as you could get without actually saying good-bye.

His father still went to work every day but came home later and later each night. When he was home, he acted confused or disoriented. Danny, searching for Bunserati's rabbit pellets in the basement, once found his father walking in circles in a dark corner near the water heater. He jumped when he saw Danny. He was looking for something, he said—canned peaches or garlic cloves—but to Danny he looked as if he'd been lost down there for a while. Another time Danny found him sitting on the bed in Simon's room, as if he were waiting for Simon to come back home. When he saw Danny, he stood quickly in that awkward way that looked guilty. He mumbled something and left the room.

It was during those long afternoons, sitting by himself in his room, listening for Bridget's footsteps in the hall, that Danny felt the strangeness of his new life most acutely. The absence of his parents, in particular, was hard to get used to. It was like noticing that the furnace was fixed because it didn't rumble and shake so much when it went on at night. The surprise wasn't in that it was fixed, but in that the noise had become so common that the *lack* of it felt different. That was how it felt with his parents so often away. It wasn't that he missed them as much as that he felt surprised that he actually was used to their being there.

What most worried Danny, though, was his father's garden.

Wade Parsons, produce man, sometime chef, was known perhaps best of all for being a master gardener. His garden, planted on the south side of the barn, was unlike any garden anyone had ever seen. It had everything imaginable and a lot of things no one would ever think to imagine. There were seven types of tomatoes alone. And on the far side, four varieties of corn. He'd planted three varieties of peppers, five of onions, and so many different kinds of squash that Danny couldn't begin to keep them straight. He'd planted peas and beans, potatoes and lettuces. He'd planted everything. And there wasn't a garden like it within five hundred miles.

But over the past few weeks, and especially after the announcement of the family's separation, the garden wilted right in front of their eyes. Weeds sprang up in every corner, choking the squash, dragging down the tomato vines, covering the lettuces. Insects ate through most of the corn, gnawed holes in the bean leaves until they turned black and fell off. The paths that ran between sections became overgrown with crabgrass, and half of the markers he'd carefully placed to identify each variety and row had fallen in the rain, become covered with dirt and overgrowth until they were lost entirely. No one ever went in there; no one picked the ripe vegetables. The garden just sat in the sun and baked and smelled like a heap of compost left too long in the back of a truck. And nobody cared.

And every day, Danny would pass the garden as he walked back from the barn. He'd smell the sharp stench of overripeness, and he'd shake his head and try to remember which life was his *real* life. In a lot of ways, his father in the barn felt a lot more real, whereas his old life felt more and more like something he'd made up, like something he'd dreamed.

13

Danny stood with the whip in his hand.

"You really do have a gift, you know," his father said from behind his shoulder. "You remind me of my friend Jerome. The first time he held this whip, it was like he was born for it." He looked at Danny more closely. "That's a strange thing, to see that someone is *born* for something. It almost never happens."

Danny's head swam. It was as if his father had reached into his heart and touched the very thing that mattered most to him in the world. *What were you born to do, Danny Parsons?*

"It's funny," his father continued. "Our purpose—what we're *supposed* to be—it sits in us like a piece of sand in an oyster, and we work it and work it in our own way. If we're lucky, we get a pearl. Not many people are that lucky."

"Are you still looking?"

Danny's father took the whip from him and looped it

in his hand. "I look every day. I never stop looking for who I'm supposed to be."

"But you know it isn't a guy in a grocery store," Danny said, laughing.

His father didn't laugh in return. He stared at the whip. "I don't know if that's true, either. I don't know a lot, although Jerome did everything he could to help me."

"Your friend from high school?"

"My best friend. We graduated together, he went to Stanford and I went to Harvard, and then, about fifteen years ago, he took me to Tibet. Ever hear of it?"

Hear of it? Danny wanted to say. *Just ask me. Gross national product, major crops, population, borders, religion.* He knew almost everything about it. It had been one of the most exotic places he'd ever imagined being from. But he just nodded at his father.

"Jerome's still there."

"In Tibet?"

His father nodded. "He's a Buddhist monk. He lives in one of those remote Himalayan monasteries that the Chinese government leaves alone."

Danny sat on a bale staring at his father. The afternoon light behind him was strong, and he almost glowed. *Could this really be my father?* he thought. *Could it?* "But you came home?" he asked.

His father laughed. "I don't think I was supposed to be a monk. When Jerome gave me this whip, he meant for me to understand that I was supposed to be something else. I like to think of it as a metaphor. In one object, so many things are expressed. It is power, it is the opener of doors, it is the creator of order. Mostly, though, I just like using it."

"So what happened when you came home?"

"I've told you all this before," his father said, smiling.

No you haven't, no you haven't, Danny screamed in his head. "Tell me again," he said. "Please."

Danny's father hung the whip on a nail on a center post of the barn and sat across from him. "I came back to finish my graduate degree. Met your mother. Moved to the family farm. Worked at the SuperValu for a while, then moved on to other things—more interesting things. Some livestock management, worked the county fair circuit operating the Tilt-A-Whirl, taught English at a prep school, opened a video store, did all kinds of things." He paused and rubbed his head. "I don't know," he said, "I kept trying things out, hoping I'd 'find myself,' I guess, but it didn't work out like I thought it would."

"But you had a family."

"Yes." He smiled. "You and your brother."

But not Bridget, Danny thought. "Tell me about after I was born."

His father looked at him curiously. "Why do you want to know that?"

"I don't know. I guess I've just never heard you talk about it."

His father paused and rubbed his head again, so that he looked just like the father Danny had always known. "That was a hard time for me, for your mother, for us all."

"Did you go away?"

His father had pulled a long strand of straw from the bale he was sitting on, and he peeled it into strips as he talked. He looked at the straw and not at Danny. "I met someone," he said. "Someone who reminded me so much of Jerome and of myself and who I had once been that"—he glanced quickly at Danny and then back at the piece of straw—"well, I was a little confused."

"A woman?"

"How'd you guess?"

Danny shrugged. "I watch TV. That helps sometimes. So what happened?"

"We went to find Jerome. About six months after you were born. I left your mother in a terrible place. It's one of the reasons she left me for the professor."

The professor? Who could that be? And more importantly, Danny thought, how much of this life and his other life overlapped?

"But you didn't stay in Tibet."

His father shook his head. "No. Jerome saw what I'd done and he was angrier than I'd ever seen him. He said he didn't know me, that I didn't know myself. He was probably right." He stared at the straw again. "Then he gave me that whip and told me to go home."

"Did you?"

"I'm here, aren't I?" He tried to smile. "But I couldn't ever make things right with your mother. You and your brother came to live with me. She started over. And that's how things have been between us. Two separate lives." He looked at his hands, then rubbed his head—habits so familiar to Danny that it gave him chills to watch this father do them. How different *were* his two fathers?

"You know, Dan, there's a lot I've screwed up over the years.

"You mean with Mom?"

"With your mom, yes, and with Jerome, too. I went back when I learned he was sick. I brought medicine I knew he would need. And he never forgave me."

"Forgave you for what?"

"For abandoning you."

"Why? We're okay."

"It's deeper than that. Jerome believed I'd betrayed the most important virtues. He thought that I'd made everything we'd learned into a lie."

"Like being the water?"

"And finding order in the chaos. And tending your garden where it blooms."

"But how?" Danny asked.

His father shook his head. "I could never figure it out. And all I had was this whip. Jerome gave it to me because he believed it would help me, I think. And it has, but probably not in the way he intended."

"What do you mean?"

"The whip has power. It flows and moves like water. But mostly, if you know what you're doing, it strikes. It has this force, this energy, and that isn't something you can ignore. It has—how should I put this?—*influence.* You want to bring order to chaos, just pull out a ten-foot bullwhip. That puts the world right in order. So that's what I do. But it isn't exactly in keeping with the teachings of a monastery."

134

Danny laughed. "I bet not."

His father's smile faded. "But I still think I've disappointed him—Jerome. And I know I've disappointed your mother. And you and Simon, too."

"How?"

"By doing this," he said, holding his arms out, encompassing the barn, the whip, the cans, everything.

"You mean instead of working at the SuperValu?"

His father stood suddenly and began pacing. "Oh, Dan, I don't know if you can understand this." He stopped pacing with his back to Danny and spoke into the walls of the barn. "The truth is, I believe it was that stupid SuperValu job that really ended things between your mother and me. She wanted me to keep it. We needed the money. But I just couldn't. I had to wear that ridiculous jumpsuit and I couldn't stand it. It was humiliating to work there. A Harvard education and I'm polishing apples? No." He turned to Danny. "You understand that, don't you? You understand why I couldn't have the whole town staring at me like I was some freak or a nobody—a guy who had nothing but a crummy job and some washed-up, pie-in-the-sky dreams. You see that, don't you?"

"Sure," Danny said. He thought of Sarah Evans, and he knew exactly what his father was describing.

His father smiled. "A guy with a whip shouldn't be trimming heads of lettuce and stacking bananas, should he?"

Danny smiled back, but inside he felt all twisted and confused. There were parts of this life that he longed for. It was powerful and it was full of potential. He felt proud to look like this man, and he hadn't felt proud like that in a long time.

"We've got something here, don't we?" his father

asked. "Something special. I see a future together, Dan. You and I taking on the world. Do you feel it, too?"

Danny nodded. He could feel it, and it felt real.

"Think of the places we could go," his father continued. "Kiwi Islands, Japan, Hong Kong."

Danny smiled. This was a conversation he'd been waiting his whole life to have. "Katmandu," he said. "Prague, Addis Ababa, Sydney."

"Johannesburg," his father added. "São Paulo, Kolkata, Hartford."

"Hartford?"

His father laughed. "Just testing you." He sat beside Danny. "You and me. And a whole world to explore. Cambodia and Indonesia."

"Turkey and Kazakhstan."

"Madagascar and Nigeria."

"Canada."

"Our first stop." His father laughed. "The first place we go is Canada."

Danny laughed, too.

And then his father reached out and grabbed him around the shoulders, pulling him close. "You and me together," he said, squeezing. "We'll be quite a team."

And for a moment, Danny completely believed it. He and his father would be a team.

But then he thought of his other life—the life that had become a dream, a bad dream. He thought of his father, wandering around, lost, his mother, who was walking alone through open doors. And he thought of Bridget.

What would it mean to follow this father with the whip? Would it mean never seeing Bridget again?

He knew that he couldn't tell Bridget about this reality.

Bridge would ask questions. She would want to know how he felt, what he was thinking. He didn't *know* how he felt. He didn't *know* what he was thinking.

Except he did, and that was the worst part about it.

Because he knew, down deep, that if he had to choose today, he would choose power and potential. He would choose the possible admiration of a dark-haired girl. He would choose a father who made him proud. And part of him believed that by choosing *this* dad, he would also be saving his other dad. If they were the same, then he was helping his father live the life he *should* have lived.

He wasn't just choosing for himself. He was choosing for his father, too.

But he couldn't admit that to Bridget. He couldn't admit that he had not chosen *her.*

And now he was about to make a choice that she would *never* make. How could he do that? What was he thinking?

"I have to go," he said, rising from the bale.

"I understand," his father said. "Come back soon?"

Danny nodded. "Sure."

He left the shadow of the barn and walked past the garden. He felt that there was a good chance he would *never* tell Bridget about this reality, this father.

And then, the very next day, he let the truth slip.

14

Bridget's room was bright that Sunday. Danny hadn't seen her in more than a day and they were retracing their steps to see if they could figure out how it was that their paths had crossed without either of them knowing about it. Bridget had wandered into the Cunningham field reading a book on the Big Bang, and it had taken her several hours to get her bearings. But at the same time, Danny had been riding his bike in that very area, looking for her. They'd never seen each other, and they couldn't figure out how that could be. It wasn't a very big field.

"Ever consider chaining yourself to your bed or attaching a long rubber band to your leg and Bunserati's cage?"

"Very funny," she said.

"We should probably feed him," Danny said. "I haven't been down there for days."

"Me either," she said. "Let's go now."

Danny and Bridget rose to go, but just as they reached

the door, they heard a car pulling up the driveway. The Parsons rarely had visitors, and Danny and Bridget ran to the window to see who it might be. It was a police cruiser. The windows were up, but they could see a figure huddled in the backseat. It looked like Simon.

"Uh-oh," Danny said.

Bridget was out the door before he turned around. "Hurry up, Danny," she called from the stairs.

When he reached the porch, his father was already talking with the officer, and his mother was leaning into the police cruiser. It *was* Simon. Their mother opened the door and led him from the car into the house. Simon followed willingly, though he refused to be touched by her. Bridget and Danny turned and watched them pass. Simon smiled at them. "Beats having to pay insurance so I can drive myself." He laughed.

But his mother was not smiling. "I don't know what this is about, young man, but you might as well start coming to terms with the fact that your summer is *over*. Into the house," she ordered.

"House arrest," he smiled, calling back to Danny and Bridget. "Beats working at the SuperValu."

Danny watched them enter the house. His mother deliberately slammed the screen door.

Bridget had Danny by the sleeve and was tugging at him. "Are you coming or what?"

Their father was shaking hands with the officer when they approached. They stood to the side and watched, careful to get close enough so that they could hear everything but not so close that they might be noticed. "Well, John," their father was saying, "I'm sorry you had to come all the way out here for something like this." He spoke as if they were friends. They stopped shaking hands and their father added, "Things have been a little unusual around here lately. We're all adjusting to some changes in our life and it's been difficult for us."

"Not a problem, Wade," the officer said. "I know things are in"—he paused, trying to settle on a word—"transition for you. That's tough. I just wanted you to know we'd been seeing a lot of Simon in town and we were getting a little concerned. Thought you might be, too."

"Yes. Very much so." Their father rubbed his head and looked at his shoes. Then he turned to Bridget and Danny. "John, do you know my other children?"

Bridget took a few steps forward, dragging Danny with her.

"Pleasure to meet you," the officer said, turning to them. He had that awkward look most adults get when they have to make conversation with young people, as if he suddenly doubted whether he'd ever been a child. In his eyes, they could see that he was debating whether they were too young to shake hands with.

"This is Bridget, and Danny," their father said, pointing to each of them. They each stuck out a hand to be shaken. "Bridget, Danny, I'd like you to meet Officer John Stevens."

"Bridget," the officer said, turning to her, "your name sounds familiar. Have I seen your picture in the paper? Something connected to the college?"

"I've been accepted into the Youth Scholarship Academy," she said.

"That's right," he said, smiling. "You're something like the youngest student ever, aren't you?"

Bridget blushed. "I think so."

"Good for you. And Danny," he said, turning to him. "What do you do?"

It was a question someone asked an adult, and Danny stood there for a moment unsure about how to respond. *I crack a bullwhip,* he thought. *I touch formulas and things explode.* Where to begin? But instead he said, "I'm going into eighth grade."

"Great," Officer Stevens said, clearly relieved that introductions were over.

"Officer Stevens is the brother of Jerome Stevens," their father announced, "my very best friend from high school."

"That's right," Officer Stevens said. "Your dad and I go way back."

"Jerome from the picture in the living room?" Bridget asked.

"That's the one," her father said.

"Crazy Ohm," Officer Stevens said, shaking his head. "He walked off the face of the earth so he could 'be the water,' or whatever it was he was always talking about. I loved that kid, but I never understood him."

Their father smiled a little sadly. "He heard his own music, didn't he?" He looked at his shoes again.

"You can say that again. The way that kid lived. And to think he almost dragged my sister, Julie, into that mess, too." The officer turned toward their father. "I'm glad you helped put a stop to that, although it would've been nice if you could've done more."

Their father nodded but didn't speak.

"Well, Wade," the officer said, holding out his hand again. "I should be getting back."

They shook one last time. "Thanks again, John. Simon won't trouble you anymore."

"No trouble," he said. "Just looking out for him."

"I appreciate it."

"So long, kids," the officer said as he pulled out of the driveway. He waved and Bridget waved back. The three of them stood and watched the dust rise behind his car until he turned onto the road that led back into town.

Their father took a deep breath. He looked tired. He checked his watch as if there were somewhere he needed to be.

"Dad?" The sound of Bridget's voice startled them all. "Why did Officer Stevens call his brother that name?"

"Ohm," he said.

"Yeah, Ohm," Bridget said.

Their father smiled. "Jerome was my best friend, and one of the holiest people I've ever known." He paused. "How can I explain this to you?" He looked at his feet again, his face troubled in a way that seemed to settle over his brow. Then he looked up again. "Jerome and I were friends for years. I always knew he was different. I guess everybody did. For one thing, he had strange ideas about personal hygiene. He only bathed once a week, for example. And he kept his head shaved. And he was interested in lots of things that nobody really understood—things like Eastern religions and astronomy and philosophy—deep things that you only study if you want your view of the world to be changed. And his was. Nobody saw the world quite the way Jerome did."

He looked at the sky suddenly and closed his eyes as if he'd been looking for something in the air and then thought he'd find it inside himself instead. "Becoming a Buddhist when he was seventeen was just the next step," he continued, "but it sealed his fate in town. Everybody thought he was the strangest thing they'd ever seen." He smiled. "He did some things that people thought were really weird. He dedicated himself to constant meditation— in class, at pep rallies, during study halls. He ignored his calculus and his biochem labs and sat in the corner of study hall and whispered mantras to himself. I remember being in exams, trying like mad to figure out the problems on a test, and hearing this quiet 'ohm' from the corner of the room where Jerome sat."

"Ohm?" Danny asked.

His father nodded. "It's a meditation mantra. You say it over and over again to clear your head by focusing on your breathing and by trying to connect with something called the Buddha essence. The idea is to let everything else fall away. Jerome said the goal is to become like the water: all-giving, all-nourishing, passive and calm and deep and powerful. It's a pretty intense idea, and Jerome"—he smiled again—"well, Jerome was a pretty intense kid."

"So that's where it comes from," Bridget said. "'Be the water.' It's from Jerome."

"Yes. He said it all the time, meditated on it, *lived* it." Their father paused. "Of course, everybody laughed at him, started calling him Ohm instead of Jerome. Even his family laughed. Nobody really understood him."

"But you did," Danny said.

His father looked at him strangely. There seemed to be a question on his lips, but he didn't ask it. "I did, I think," he said. "Not entirely, but a little."

"Is that why Officer Stevens said that thing about the way he lived?" Bridget asked.

"Yes. To the people in town, it looked like Jerome didn't believe in anything. There wasn't any visible order to his life, really. He just lived. His life *looked* like it was nothing but chaos"—Danny felt Bridget shoot him a look—"but inside he was living a deeply ordered life." He looked at the sky again, searching for something. "That was the other thing he used to say. He believed that on the surface, life can look like a mess. The secret is to make the mess into a maze. For Jerome, there wasn't any such thing as chaos. Chaos wasn't chaos, it was just the natural imposition of a *different* kind of order—a kind we aren't yet able to understand. And that's what he was trying to do, I think. Find the secret to the disorder in the world, find the secret that would make the mess into a maze."

"Did he?"

"I don't know."

They were all silent for a moment, but Danny's mind felt like it would explode. Then Bridget asked the question. "How did he die?"

"We graduated from high school together. Jerome graduated top of the class, which made people crazy, too. All that meditation in study halls and chanting 'ohm' during tests, and he still aced everything they gave him. He was brilliant."

"What number were you?" Bridget asked.

"I was number two, and that was only because I studied like crazy just to keep up."

"So what happened?" Danny asked.

"Well, he went to Stanford and I went to Harvard. We kept in pretty close touch, but after a few years he decided that college wasn't for him. So he sold everything he owned and went to Tibet, hiking through the Himalayas from Buddhist monastery to monastery, tracking snow leopards and reading the works of Master Dogen and the Dalai Lama. That's where he died, in Tibet."

"The picture in the living room. That's you two in Tibet, isn't it?" Danny asked.

"Yes." Their father looked at his shoes, then up at the sky again, and breathed in deeply. He let the air out quickly. "That was the last time I saw him."

"When was it?"

"Oh, let's see . . . thirteen, almost fourteen years ago. Danny, you weren't even born yet, but you were on the way, and I knew I had to see him before you came. I had a sense my life would change so much—my life already *had* changed so much. I was finishing a graduate degree, I'd met your mother and we'd been married and had Simon. If I didn't see Jerome then, I feared I'd never see him again. And your mother and I agreed it was the best time to go. So I went. I was with him for three months, and it was incredible."

"It looks beautiful there," Bridget said.

"It was, but it was more than that for me. He invited me into the monastery, and as soon as I stepped into the compound, I felt like I'd found a reason to live—when I hadn't even known I'd needed one. For my whole life, I'd been wandering, searching, trying to find a path that made sense. I didn't find purpose at Harvard."

"You found it in Tibet," Bridget said.

He smiled. "That's right. Or I thought I'd found it. I wrote your mother a very long, very difficult letter about it, and it made her very angry."

"Why?" Bridget asked.

"Because she saw it as a betrayal, which it was. I told her I had found something that I had to follow, but it meant that I wouldn't be coming home. In her mind, I'd chosen Jerome over her. I'd chosen a spiritual life over emotional attachment. I'd chosen myself over my children. And I guess I had."

"But you came home," Danny said. "Why?"

"Jerome made me. He said I hadn't found *my* path. He said I was pretending and only really traveling *his* path. He told me I had to tend my garden where it bloomed, and it wasn't blooming in Tibet. And then I told him I'd written that letter and he was furious. He said I hadn't learned anything. And then he asked me to leave. So I did."

"Were things okay with Mom?" Bridget asked.

"We had a lot of work to do to get past that letter I'd written," he said. "But we put our life back together, more or less. Danny, you came along and that changed everything again. We were just hanging on, I think. And that's when I got the letter from the monastery."

"About Jerome?" Bridget asked.

He nodded. "Actually, *I* didn't get the letter. His family did. They didn't know what to do, so they came to me."

"Julie," Bridget said.

He smiled. "Yes. Julie was Jerome's sister. She's the one who brought me the letter. And that created a whole bunch of new problems."

"Was she pretty?" Bridget asked.

"Very," he said. "And more than that, she reminded me so much of her brother, it was almost painful. She was a 'wanderer,' too, I guess. I liked that about her. She begged me to go, to travel with her to Tibet to save her brother, to save my best friend. She was *very* persuasive."

"But you didn't go," Danny said.

His father shook his head.

"Why?" Danny asked.

"Partly because I knew he didn't want me there. Partly because of you and Simon. But mostly I didn't go because I didn't get the chance."

"What do you mean?" Bridget asked.

"I was going to go," he said.

"You *were*?"

He nodded slowly. "I was. I'd told your mother. I'd made the arrangements."

"She had a new baby and you were going to *leave* her?" Bridget said. "To go off with *Julie*?"

"I'm not proud of it, Bridget. I'm telling you this so you'll understand why things with your mother are so difficult."

"But you didn't go," Danny said. "Why not?"

"It's a good question," his father said. "And the truth is, I

147

didn't go because I hesitated too long. I couldn't decide. I didn't make my choice until it was too late. By the time I chose, the choice had been taken from me. Jerome had died."

"And you'd already told Mom you were leaving?" Bridget asked.

"Yes."

"But then you stayed," she said.

"Yes."

"But it didn't matter, did it? Because you hadn't chosen her."

"That's right."

The three of them were silent for a moment.

"We made it work," their father continued. "You came along soon after that, and having a third meant things had to *really* change. I left the program at Harvard because it didn't make sense anymore. We moved back here to live with your Grampa Joe. I got a job. You three grew. Time passed."

"But it was never the same," Bridget concluded.

"No." He stared at his shoes again. "And all I can think, even today, is that I might have saved him if I'd gone to Tibet."

"You would have," Danny said.

Bridget glared at him. "You don't know that," she said.

"I know," he mumbled. "I just . . ." He didn't know what to say. He'd said too much already. "I'm sorry, Dad. I didn't mean anything."

"No, it's okay. You're probably right. Still, we make choices, or we're *supposed* to make choices. I often wonder what would have happened if I'd actually chosen and acted on that choice." He looked at his children. "I have a lot of regrets," he said. "Jerome. Harvard. This mess I made with your mom. A lot of things."

"Do you miss him?" Danny asked.

"I miss him every day, Danny."

"He sounds amazing," Bridget said.

"He was. And in the end, staying was the right decision. I just wish it was a decision I had *made.*"

They were silent again.

"So you never did see him again," Danny asked.

"No. But he left a will. He didn't have a thing in the world to his name that was really *worth* anything, but that crazy holy man left a will. And he gave everything he had to me—which was basically nothing, or most people would think so. But I treasure his belongings. And in a way I guess Jerome still guides me."

"What did he give you?" Bridget asked.

"Oh, nothing really. His books, his journals, a prayer wheel that a monk had given him when he first arrived, and a leather whip that somehow got lost in transit. I never could track it down."

The whip. Danny almost choked. "But how . . . ," he began.

Bridget turned to him. "How what?" she asked. Her eyes were narrowed again, sharp and piercing like lasers that could bore into him.

"I was just thinking. . . ." Then he shook his head. "Never mind."

15

Minutes later, after Danny had returned to his room, Bridget burst through the door without knocking. "How did you know that stuff about Jerome?" she asked.

Danny stammered and hesitated.

"Out with it, Danny Parsons."

He'd been holding this secret for weeks, and now here was Bridget, his best friend in the world, the one who knew him better than anyone, asking him directly. He paused. He tried desperately to think of a lie, anything, but nothing came. Nothing. "Dad told me," he blurted.

"He did not. How did you know?"

Danny picked at a loose thread on his comforter. "I've been talking with him," he began. "In the barn."

"And?"

He felt as if he were standing on the edge of a cliff, and he steadied himself for the jump. "Only it isn't him. Not exactly."

"What are you talking about?" she said.

"I meet him in the barn."

"The formula," she whispered to herself. "Take me there now," she said to Danny.

"You've already been there. That first day I had the formula, when you couldn't find me, I was in the barn."

"No, you weren't. I checked the barn."

"I know. You couldn't see us."

"Could you see me?"

"No."

"But that's impossible, unless . . ." Her brow furrowed in concentration. She pushed her glasses up with one hand and grabbed a shock of hair with the other. "No," she mumbled, shaking her head, "it can't be." She turned to him and narrowed her eyes. "What else are you hiding from me, Danny Parsons?"

"Nothing."

"You liar."

He sighed and lowered his head. She was going to figure it out sooner or later and that would be worse. Plus it was all getting too complicated, and he couldn't figure it out on his own.

"Out with it!" she demanded.

"Fine." He turned toward her and blurted it out. "He doesn't know you."

"Who doesn't?"

"Dad in the barn. He never knew you. In his world"— his voice got quiet—"in his world you don't exist."

She stood there for a full minute. Danny thought she

was going into shock or something, and he reached out to touch her, but she pulled away from him.

"I can't believe you've been hiding this from me," she said, fury in her eyes.

"I didn't know what to do. I knew it had to do with the formulas, and, I don't know, I guess I was afraid to lose him."

"You could lose a lot more than that." She shook her head. "You've made a huge mess, Danny. Do you know that?"

"How is this my fault?"

She shook her head again. "My room. Now."

"Yes, ma'am," he mumbled.

In her room, Bridget went straight for her notebook. Danny stood obediently next to her desk and waited. It was a little embarrassing to be standing next to his sister's desk as if she were his teacher and he were about to lose recess privileges. "Can I just remind everyone here that you're not even a teenager and I am?"

She looked at him, her face completely blank. Just like a teacher. "Your point is?"

"Nothing," he mumbled.

She turned toward him and stared into his eyes. "Listen to me," she said. "Are you listening?"

"Yes."

"He isn't your father, Danny. Do you get that?"

He stared at the floor. *Yes, he is,* he said to himself. *He is my father.* But he said nothing to Bridget. He just stared at the floor while she continued to shoot him the look of unforgivable disappointment.

"What?" he finally burst out. "Why are you looking at me like that?"

She shook her head. "It's worse than I thought," she mumbled.

"What are you talking about?"

She tore a sheet of paper from the notebook and pulled a pencil from her drawer. "More pictures," she said. "Pay attention."

Danny's stomach started to churn with worry. Part of it was the math phobia that often accompanied these discussions with Bridget. Part of it was the humiliation of having to be taught things by his sister, though, he had to admit, it didn't bother Simon that much. But the biggest part of Danny's worry had to do with the man in the barn who would be his father, who was his father. It was the fear that Danny might lose him somehow.

If Bridget sensed his anxiety, she ignored it. She was all business. "Remember what I told you about the uncertainty principle?"

He nodded. "Wave, particle, but they aren't both or they *are* both or . . . I don't remember."

"They *are* both, but we can't *know* them as both. We can't *measure* them as both. We can know where an electron is or how fast it's going, but not both."

"That's it. I remember."

"Okay. Well, watch this." She drew a circle with wavy lines in it. "What is this?" she asked.

He almost said a bucket of water, but then he remembered seeing it before. "I know! It's an electron in a bucket."

"Yes. Now watch." She drew a line down the middle of the bucket.

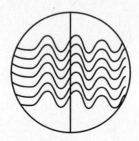

"Imagine that I put a piece of metal right down the middle of the bucket so that the two sides were completely separated. Now where's the electron?"

Danny stared at the drawing. How was he supposed to know? "I don't know," he said. "Over here or over there," he guessed, pointing first to one side and then the other.

"Wrong."

"Very funny, Bridget."

"I'm not joking."

"Then where is it?"

"It's in *both sides.*"

He was starting to lose patience. *It's fine to spend half a summer learning science and math,* he thought, *but now she's going too far.* "Knock it off, B. I mean it."

"I'm not joking."

"How is it in both places? It's just one electron, isn't it?"

"Yes. But this isn't like the real world that we're used to. This is the quantum world, and in the quantum world—"

"Things work differently." He completed the sentence for her.

"That's right," she said. "The quantum world is so unpredictable, in this case we can't even guess. It's so unpredictable that, according to the laws of the quantum world, the electron literally exists in both places. Until we look."

"I don't get it."

"Okay. Here's another example. There was a scientist named Schrödinger, and he created this imaginary experiment with a cat." She flipped the paper over as she spoke and drew a box. Inside the box she drew a stick figure of a cat, a hammer, two smaller boxes, and a small bottle. "He imagined a cat in a sealed box. Inside the box he also put a hammer, a bottle of poisonous acid, a small piece of unstable matter, and a Geiger counter. You with me?"

"A Geiger counter is . . . ?"

"A device that measures radioactivity."

"Got it."

"Okay," she said. "This is how it worked. He imagined closing up the box and waiting. That bit of unstable matter could break down, and if it did, it would release a single electron. If that happened, the electron would register on the Geiger counter, which would trigger a switch that would release the hammer, smashing the bottle. Poisonous gas would go everywhere and the cat would die."

"Cool." Danny had no special love for cats.

"But it was just as likely that the matter wouldn't degrade and release an electron. Then nothing would strike the Geiger counter, no switch would be triggered, no hammer, no smashing, no dead cat."

"Yeah? So?"

"So you can't know which it is until you look. And,

155

according to the laws of the quantum world, until you look, *both* cats exist in the box—a live one and a dead one. Until you look, they *both* exist. Schrödinger called it superposition. Both cats exist in a state of superposition, and when you look, one becomes real and the other sort of disappears."

"I still don't get it."

She smiled and almost laughed. "I don't really, either, to tell you the truth. But it's true. All the math says so."

Danny stared at the paper and tried to get his mind to understand something that didn't actually make any sense. Until you look, both exist. What did that mean?

And yet something about it troubled him. Because there was a man in the barn with a whip and there was a man in a green SuperValu uniform in the kitchen and they both existed. They both existed.

And then it hit him. This wasn't some arbitrary science lesson. Bridget wasn't hoping to raise his SAT scores. This was about his *life*. He was actually living in a—what did Bridget call it?—a state of superposition. That was it. He was living in a state of superposition. Both cats existed, both fathers existed.

"Until you look?" he mumbled.

"Yes," she said, turning to him. She stared up into his eyes, and even as he avoided her gaze he could see her, the way she looked, the way she, too, worried. "You see why this is such a mess?"

He nodded. "I'm seeing them both, aren't I?"

"Yes."

"Why? Why me?"

"That's a good question, and we have to figure it out *now*."

"Wow. Okay. This is very weird," he said. He would have started pacing, but there were too many things to step over. "What should I do? What do you want me to do? Want me to carry another formula around?" he asked.

"First of all, calm down," she said. "What did you *think* was happening? You have a father in the barn who isn't your father. Didn't that worry you before?"

"I haven't really thought about it."

She shook her head. "You haven't thought about it." Then she glared at him one last time. "You can't see him anymore."

"What do you mean?"

"In the barn. You can't see him again. You have to stay out of there."

"Why?"

"Because to *see* is to *measure*. To *see* is to *choose,* to *know*. One of the cats exists, and we find out which one by looking. *One* of these fathers exists, and you'll determine which one by *seeing* him. You can't see that other father again."

"Okay."

"I mean it, Danny."

"I know."

"Because to see him is . . ." She breathed quickly and stared at the paper in front of her.

"Is not to see you," he said, finishing her sentence.

"Exactly." Then she turned to him. "And don't you *ever* keep something like this from me again. Do you understand?"

He nodded. "Sorry."

"And you promise you won't see him again?"

"Yes," he lied.

"Good. Now let me get back to work. We've got a mess on our hands. It's all starting to make sense, and it scares me to death, Danny." She turned to him. "It scares me to death."

He nodded. But he was thinking of something else. He was thinking of the feel of a whip in his hands. He was thinking of a life of possibility. He was thinking of dreams coming true.

He watched Bridget work and thought of his father in the barn, and as he did, the strangest thing started to happen. There were moments when Bridget's fingers, clamped around the pencil, looked normal. But there were moments when it looked as if the pencil hovered over the page all by itself. She was there beside him, and then, for a moment, she was gone. He had promised not to keep things from Bridget, but he'd broken that promise as soon as he'd made it. He *would* see his father in the barn. He *had* to.

And he would break his promise again. Because standing there next to Bridget, he saw something he could *never* tell her. It was something he couldn't even admit to himself.

It looked as if Bridget was disappearing.

Both fathers couldn't exist once the box was opened. Both worlds couldn't exist once the box was opened.

And the box was going to have to be opened eventually.

16

Danny went to his room and wandered from one shelf to the next. Nothing could hold his attention. *National Geographic* didn't interest him; his maps and notebooks seemed almost silly. He'd never felt such restless discontent before, except maybe in math class.

Through his window he could see the shadows cast by the setting sun as it struck the stand of tall pines beyond the barn. The barn. He thought of his father in there, moving the whip and making plans for a life of adventure, a life of possibilities, a life that was so much more than the dreams Danny had been making up for himself. It was a life of actually living the things he'd read about in *National Geographic*. And they'd made plans. There were so many things they might do. The possibilities made Danny practically itch with longing. He felt caged suddenly, like Bunserati, locked in a wire box behind the barn. And suddenly he just had to get out.

But at the edge of the barn, in the garden, something caught his eye.

At first he thought it was a raccoon foraging for something ripe and tasty. But when he saw the flash of light off metal, he knew it was something else. He thought of his father, but that seemed unlikely. His father hadn't been in the garden for weeks.

Then he caught a glimpse through a break in the sunflowers of a red and white baseball jersey. Number eight. That was Simon's number. It had to be him.

Danny tried to imagine what Simon would be doing in the garden. He might be gathering a snack before dinner, but he moved through the garden too quickly to be grazing. He wasn't stopping to gather and munch. This was something else.

Danny saw him raise his arm, and in a flash of silver the leaves of a cucumber plant fell to the ground. Simon raised his arm again and leveled a tomato plant. He was swinging one of their father's chopping knives. Their father kept them very sharp, and Simon was using one to slash and destroy just about everything he passed. Pepper plants were leveled, the heads of sunflowers were gone, cornstalks bowed over as if they'd been punched in the stomach. He was destroying the garden.

Danny rushed to Bridget's room.

"Bridget," he panted as he entered the room, practically out of breath. "B, you've got to see what's happening"—but then he stopped.

Bridget was at her desk, just where he expected her to be. Her lamp was on and the space within the light reminded him of their mother's desk in the shed—a circle of light and order in the sprawl and mess around her.

On the bed across from her, wearing a number eight jersey and tapping the crumbs from a breakfast bar wrapper into his mouth, sat Simon.

"S-Simon," Danny said, stammering. "What are you—?"

Bridget looked up at him and stared. Simon chewed and stared into the wrapper. Then he glanced over at Danny quickly, looking at him as if he was wondering whether Danny had gone crazy.

"What brings you back so quickly?" Bridget asked. "Get lonely?"

Danny couldn't stop staring at Simon. "What are you doing here?" he asked.

"We're just talking," Bridget said for Simon, because his mouth was full.

Simon swallowed. "Yeah," he said. "Just talking. What's the matter?"

"Nothing," Danny said. "I just thought I saw you in the garden. There was someone in the garden just now wearing that shirt." He pointed to Simon's jersey.

"Really?" Simon asked, looking around for something else to eat.

"Yeah," Danny said. "It was number eight."

Simon laughed. "Weird," he said. He licked his finger and rubbed it on a sticky patch of juice that had dried on Bridget's headboard. Then he licked his finger again. Danny thought he might just lean over and lick the wood with his tongue. He'd never seen Simon look so hungry.

And he'd never seen Bridget look so out of it. Her eyes

stared across the room at a collection of posters—Galaxy M100, the Horsehead Nebula, the Andromeda Galaxy— but she wasn't looking at them. Danny could tell by the fact that she never blinked once the whole time Simon licked the sticky thing on her bed. She just got all glassy-eyed in that sort of dazed, lost way that cartoon characters get just before they fall over. Danny could almost see the stars circling her head.

"You all right?" he asked her.

She shook her head quickly as if to snap herself out of something. "I'm fine," she said. "I'm thinking. This is what thinking looks like."

"You looked like you'd seen a ghost," he said.

"Yeah," Simon said. "You sure you're all right, B?"

"Would you stop it? I'm *fine*. It's called *thinking*. You two may not recognize it, but it's something that normal people do all the time. So could we not talk about it like it's a medical condition?"

"Yeah, sure," Simon said. "I gotta go, anyway. I think it's time for dinner or something." He smiled in such a leering, greedy way that Danny reached into his pocket and pulled out a Fig Newton. It was almost instinctive. *Give him the cookie,* Danny thought, *otherwise, nobody's safe.*

"You going to eat that?" Simon asked.

Danny tossed it to him as quickly as he could without looking desperate.

"Thanks," Simon said, moving toward the door. "See ya, B."

Bridget just stared at him as he closed the door.

"Is this like with the cats in the box?" Danny asked.

"I think so."

"But I don't *understand,* Bridget." Danny's voice was rising and there was an edge of panic in it. "Where are these people coming from? What's going on?"

"I think I know, but it sounds so weird that I'm sort of afraid to tell you."

"I have to know."

"I know you do." She sighed. "Okay. Can I draw another picture?"

"Whatever you have to do, just do it."

She took her acceptance letter from the top of the pile on her desk and turned it over. With a pink highlighter, she drew two paths that moved away from each other at a ninety-degree angle. Then she drew a line across them near the top.

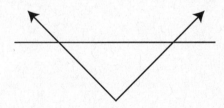

"The problem all along," she said, "has been the uncertainty principle. Scientists have been trying to outsmart an electron for years—to trick it into revealing both its position and its speed. Then a team of scientists set up this experiment. They released two identical electrons at the same time—one down one tube and one down the other. The idea was that they'd measure where the electron was in one tube and measure the speed in the other and then they'd know *both* things at the same time, and the dilemma of the uncertainty principle would be solved."

"That's a good idea."

"Yeah. Except that it didn't work."

"Why not?"

"This is the weird thing. The moment the scientists measured one electron, the other electron suddenly— instantaneously—*changed*. It was as if the electron being measured called to the other one to change so that the principle would still hold true."

"Can that happen?"

"Maybe. But if it did, it had to happen faster than the speed of light and that, according to Einstein and a lot of other people, is impossible."

"Then what was it?"

"Well," she said, taking a deep breath, "the only theory that actually *explains* it, the only theory that makes mathematical as well as theoretical sense, is the multiuniverse theory."

"The . . ."

"Multiuniverse theory."

"Which is?"

"Just what it sounds like. More than one universe exists. A lot more."

"Sounds like a *Star Trek* episode."

"It isn't," she said. "It's a fact. I know that now."

"Come on, Bridget. I thought you were a *real* scientist."

"I am. And this is real science." He shook his head, but she wouldn't let it go. She looked at him out of the corner of her eye as if she were sharing a secret with him. "And I think I've figured out why *you're* the key, Danny. It isn't the formulas at all, is it? It's *you*."

"I don't know what you're talking about."

"Yes, you do."

"Prove it," he said.

"I will," she said, and she smiled the way she did just before she was going to triple-jump him in checkers or put him into checkmate. She crossed her arms and legs and sat back against her chair.

"Think about how in a single morning people make a bunch of choices," she said. "Like what to eat, what to wear, whether they're going to ride their bike to school or walk. And now imagine that every time you make that choice, the universe splits: in one universe, there's you eating cereal, but another universe gets created where you're eating a bagel instead. Everything is exactly the same except for that one choice."

"Another universe?"

"Just like this one, but completely separate because of that one choice."

Danny stared at her. "Real scientists believe this?"

"Yes. In many ways, it's the only possible explanation for the experiment I just told you about. The electrons didn't *communicate*. It wasn't that. It was the *scientists* who changed things. They measured one electron and the universe changed—a change that changed the *other* electron so that it couldn't be measured the same way. Every time we choose, that same thing happens: the universe divides. We're here with our choice, but somewhere else, in another dimension, we're living with the *other* choice."

"That doesn't prove anything."

"Of course it does. Pay attention." She grabbed a piece of paper from a drawer in her desk. "Imagine that these two universes are kept separate by only one thing: the choice that you made. The choosing alone defines the quantum world, makes one world what it is and the other world what it is. But now imagine that you had to make a choice and you didn't, in fact, choose."

"Like what?"

"Like holding a photograph of your grandfather and having the dream world and the real world overlap because you haven't chosen which is real. Or like having to choose your father."

"Nobody gets to do that."

"Well," she said, "it looks like *you* do. And until you do, there's nothing separating these two worlds. They exist together."

Danny stared at her. It was true. He knew it was true. But why? "Why me?" he asked.

"I used to think it was the *measuring* that changed the quantum world," she said. "That only scientists really influenced it. But of course it's much broader than that, isn't it? The quantum world gets changed all the time. It gets changed when we eat lunch, when we bring in the garbage cans, when we do our homework. Every time someone in the world *chooses* to do something or not do something, every time someone makes any choice at all, the quantum world changes. Choosing is the same thing as looking into the box. It's that simple. Maybe the quantum world looks so random because we're choosing so often. I don't know. Or maybe it's like Jerome says. You know, that it isn't random, it isn't chaos; it's just another kind of order, a kind we don't understand. And choosing, I think, is at the center of it all. It's choosing. But you, Danny"—she looked at him hard—"you *don't* choose things."

He looked at her as if she'd said something ridiculous. What did she mean, he didn't choose things? Of course he chose things. It felt like an insult. And it hurt. "Yes, I do choose things," he said.

She shook her head. "Think about it, Danny. I know you hate to hear it, but you're just like Dad, and not just in the way you look or the way you rub your head when you're worried. You're just like him in the way that you don't *do* anything. You don't *choose* things. Neither does Dad, really. Maybe he used to, but not anymore. The world happens to you just like it happens to him."

"I do too choose."

"Name one time."

He tried to shake something sensible out of his head. "I choose . . . breakfast," he blurted, and immediately regretted it.

She almost laughed. "I put a bowl of cereal in front of you, and no matter what it is, you eat it."

"That's not true." Though he knew it was.

Then she did laugh. "We've *tested* it. I can't even *tell* you the kinds of disgusting things that Simon has put in front of you that you've just eaten without saying a word."

He hadn't known that. "Really?"

"It's not a big deal, Danny, but it does prove my point. You don't *choose*. You *dream*. You *imagine*. You live in a sea of possibilities—lives you might live, lives you're supposed to live—but you don't *choose* one. You don't choose *anything*. You never have." She shook her head. "The amazing thing is that in this case that might actually be a strength."

"How?"

"Well, it's sort of hard to explain, but you know how in the quantum world, nothing happens predictably—there are no guaranteed events? Things might happen and they might not—there's no event that is destined to happen? In human terms, that makes choice a really important element, even at the quantum level. We *choose,* and that is what shapes our reality. Are you with me?"

"I think so."

"But you don't choose, so your reality—and I'm not entirely sure about what's going on, but I think that your reality isn't being shaped anymore. What we might be seeing is some of the *possibilities* of your reality. There's a bigger choice you have to make—one that affects all the others. You just have to make your choice."

"But where did the other choices *come* from?"

"I don't know."

"Two worlds . . . ," he muttered. Just like two Simons. One of them walking around destroying things and the other eating anything that wasn't nailed down. But there was something he didn't understand. "If this is all true, it still doesn't explain why I can see both Simons. Doesn't one of them disappear when we look at the other one?"

"For me and everyone else in the family, yes. When we look, we define the reality of the Simon we're with."

She reached under a stack of books and pulled out her drawing of the cat in the box and stared at it. Then she looked up, catching Danny's eye, holding it and not letting go. She searched his face for something. Then she shook her head. "But for you, Danny, it's different," she said. "It's like you can exist inside the box. You don't choose things or change things, you just *see* them. And you can see both cats—both Simons."

"But that means that the only way to make one real is . . ."

Bridget finished his sentence for him. "Is to put them together and look to see which one is going to become the real one."

Danny turned from Bridget's stare and looked out the window. In a way, what Bridget was saying made a lot of sense. It explained why he could see his father in the barn and his father in the SuperValu suit. But that didn't mean that it was easy to really *understand*. And he had no idea what to *do* about it.

"What now?" he asked.

Silence drifted between them like a thick blanket. It

was as if the future were suddenly knowable, which, in a way, it was, and that knowing had a weight to it that they couldn't have imagined before this.

"You have to choose one."

"But it isn't that easy, is it?" Danny asked, staring at her.

"I don't know," she said. "It's easy for most of us. We do it all the time. But you're different. And this choice is different." She held her hands up to the light so that they could both see them. They had a strange translucent quality, like the way they'd looked when she was holding the pencil, there and not there at the same time. "The question is, which universe do you like best?"

And that was exactly what Danny had been thinking. It wasn't really about choosing a father, it was about choosing a world. And one world had a father who seemed amazing but who never created Bridget. The other was the life he'd been trying to get away from for years. And choosing one meant surrendering the other entirely. It would be gone, lost to him forever. He might not even remember what he'd given up. But then again, he might, and that could be even worse.

He turned to Bridget, but she was staring out the window. Voices were coming from the yard. He heard someone laugh in that sharp way that sounded almost like a bark. Then someone shouted. It sounded like Simon, and not like Simon.

Both worlds together in one world. Until someone chose one. Until someone looked in the box to see if the cat had died.

No, Danny thought. Not *someone*. *Him*. He was the one who had to choose.

"Sometimes," Bridget said, "my room isn't my room."

"What are you talking about?" he said.

She turned to him. "Sometimes it looks like nobody sleeps in my room at all. It has frilly curtains and framed watercolor paintings on the wall. It looks like a guest room. My room does. Did you know that?" He shook his head. "I call it my underroom," she said, smiling to herself. "My underroom. But it isn't my room, is it, Danny?" She continued to stare at him. "Is it?"

"Why didn't you tell me?"

"I guess we all have our little fears that we like to keep secret."

He didn't know what to say. The voices outside had been replaced by a silence that was so still and seemed so permanent that it frightened him.

She smiled sadly and put her hand on his shoulder. "Can you feel this?" she asked.

He nodded.

"That's good," she said. "I think there might come a time when you can't. Do you believe that?"

"I don't know what I believe."

"No," she said. "Sometimes I don't know, either." She smiled at him sadly. "Maybe I'll see you later," she said. And then she left.

Someone had to choose, Danny said to himself. *He* had to choose.

And he was about to make his first choice.

17

There was no family dinner that night. Neither Simon nor their mother had been present for the family dinners for days. Simon, as they'd learned, had been hanging out in town, making trouble, and their mother had moved enough furniture to her apartment to make it a "home." She was sleeping there now. Bridget had decided to spend the last three weeks of summer at the house.

But with a big chunk of the family missing, family dinner seemed to the rest of them like a pointless obligation. What was the point of family obligations if there wasn't a family? Even after Officer Stevens returned Simon to the house, their mother remained absent. That was a hole they couldn't ignore. The few times they did gather as a family, they sat in silence at the table and stared at the empty chair across from their father.

Then, without speaking about it to each other, they began eating by themselves. Instead of heading for the kitchen to concoct an edible work of genius, their father returned from work with a pizza from town and left it open on the counter for everyone to pick from. Members of the family drifted into the kitchen and either took a piece of the cold pizza or dug in the fridge for anything that hadn't already been consumed by Happy Simon. The fridge offered slim pickings, though. Almost everything was either stale or sour.

Danny decided on the pizza that night and ate in his room, sitting at his desk, where he could see out his window. He was looking for Simon, although he wasn't exactly sure what he was going to do if he saw him. There'd been no sign of Simon in the kitchen—nearly half the pizza was still there when Danny went down for a slice—and from his window he could see that the garden was quiet.

It was a still evening, the kind of twilight that feels like it's holding its breath, as if it were right on the edge of night but hadn't committed itself yet. The dusk seemed to sit between two worlds, and in that moment he could feel the day and the night existing in a precarious balance, hovering on the edge, so that if he breathed, if a single cricket chirped, night would push itself into the moment and day would never be able to get back.

Then it happened. He saw Simon heading toward the side of the barn where they kept Bunserati. He had a head of lettuce in one hand and a bag of baseballs in the other.

"Hey, Danny?" Simon called to the house. "Check it out. I've been working on my fastball. Pinpoint accuracy. Just watch." He turned toward the house and smiled that frightening Mean Simon smile that gave Danny the creeps every time he saw it. Then he laughed. "I wish Dad could see this. It'll be better than a performance with the whip."

It was warm, and all the windows in the house were open. Simon must have known this. He had to know that Danny would hear him, and that others would, too. But why would he shout to the house like that? Why would he want others to know what he was doing? Then Danny remembered that there *weren't* any others in this world. His mother was gone, and Bridget . . .

He watched Simon head for Bunserati's cage. And suddenly he knew.

He dropped the pizza and leaned across his desk. "Simon!" he screamed out the window. "Don't you dare do it! Don't do it!"

Simon laughed loudly enough for Danny to hear him from the stairs, which Danny was taking three at a time. He couldn't move fast enough.

Danny passed his father standing at the kitchen sink, a can of root beer in one hand and a fork in the other, completely oblivious to what was happening outside. He was staring at the drain as if he'd lost something in there, or as if he'd forgotten what a drain was for. Danny didn't even pause. He knocked against the kitchen chairs as he ran past and slammed into the screen, making it bounce off the porch wall.

He was out the door and into the yard in seconds, but it felt as if it was taking forever. He could almost see the air pass by him as he rushed through it. The more energy he used, the heavier he seemed to get and the more slowly he seemed to go. It was what light must feel like when it passes through a prism, he thought, and he shook his head, chasing the image and all it meant from his mind. He had to get there faster.

"Simon!" he screamed.

Simon was still calling and laughing. "You gotta see this, Dan. You gotta see this. It's like he hasn't eaten in weeks. This is going to be so great."

"No!" Danny screamed, because it was true—he hadn't fed Bunserati in a long time. The rabbit would be ravenous. He would eat anything, do anything.

Before he reached the barn, he knew it was too late.

He heard the first crash of a baseball against the side of the barn. Then another. The next sounded tinnier, a sharp rattling sound. Again, the same sound. But between the crashing sound and the tinny sound was another sound that Danny couldn't let himself imagine. It was a soft, thickly muffled *thump* that made him feel sick.

Danny finally rounded the corner of the barn and stood, hunched over slightly, catching his breath. He could see Bunserati lying in a heap beside his bowl, his ears standing up off his head as if he were surprised to find himself lying there when all he'd been thinking about was eating. Three baseballs had rolled to the corner of his cage, and one was in his bowl beside a chunk of lettuce. He was completely still, with a piece of half-eaten lettuce hanging out of the side of his mouth. Both his eyes were open and one of them was bruised and bleeding. He didn't blink. He wasn't ever going to blink again. Ever.

Simon was reaching into the cage to grab him by the neck and drag him out.

"Dan, you gotta come see this. You might even cry!"

"Why, Simon?" Danny said. His voice was so quiet, but the night took it and carried it for miles. "Why would you do this?"

Simon saw Danny out of the corner of his eye and turned to face him through the mesh walls of the cage, contorting his face into an exaggerated frown. "Boo-hoo," he said. Then he laughed.

Danny felt confused and furious and so sad that he thought he would *burst*. This wasn't the Simon he knew— or thought he knew. This Simon was changed, and there was no clearer example than this. Simon had stopped caring about Bunserati about a year ago, but he would never have done this. The old Simon—not this Mean Simon and not the Happy Simon, the old Simon who was predictable and normal—would never have done this.

But the fact was that things weren't normal, and that made Danny angrier than he'd ever felt before. Things weren't normal and he was to blame. It was *his* fault. His— not Bridget's and not these stupid formulas that he carried in his pocket. This nightmare that Simon had become, the limp and bleeding fur in the cage that had once been their rabbit, it was all his fault, all part of *his* dream. It was a terrible accident that he'd caused. And he'd caused it without meaning to, without wanting to.

Rage built inside him until he couldn't control it. It was like a hot core of darkness that kept getting larger and larger, eventually reaching the point where his body could no longer hold it. His face felt as if it were burning and he thought he might explode, might destroy himself, in a self-induced moment of spontaneous combustion. And if he was going to be destroyed, he wasn't going alone. He was taking Simon with him. He'd destroy him, the cage, maybe take the barn, too, and the entire family. He almost wished for it. And in that moment of wishing, the rage took him.

Almost half of Simon's body was inside Bunserati's cage. He was reaching into the corner to drag the rabbit out, which wasn't easy. Bunserati was the biggest rabbit any of them had ever seen, and Simon grunted with every tug. He wasn't watching Danny anymore, and that was when Danny put his head down and ran at him with all his might. Surrendering to the rage, he lowered his shoulder into Simon's ribs. Danny heard the air rush out of his brother, and the next thing he knew, they were both lying on the ground.

Danny jumped to his feet and stood over Simon, calculating the best place to kick him, wanting to make Simon hurt as much as he did. He'd taken aim at his kidneys and would kick him there as long as it took until Simon moved, exposing his stomach and chest and face. Then Danny would really go to work. He was almost blind in his rage. He brought his foot back, but then he heard Bridget shouting from the house.

"Simon!" she yelled. "Wait. Don't go!" There was the sound of a bicycle kicking up gravel and rolling down the driveway.

Danny didn't know what to do exactly, but something in him called out, *You get to choose, you get to choose,* over and over again in his head. *This is it,* he thought. He had a dead rabbit and one Simon in front of him, and it sounded as if there was another Simon taking off down the driveway.

This was Bridget's lesson all over again. Both cats were in the box waiting for someone to look at them—to choose. Then and only then would the cats become just one cat. The same thing had to be true for the Simons. *If this is like the quantum world,* he thought, *and we're all inside the box, then both exist in that—what did Bridget call it, again?—that state of superposition.* But if Danny could see them both together, then they couldn't *both* exist like that. They'd each have to become something *real.* Seeing them would make one of them real. The other one, like the other cat or like the wavy lines in the bucket, would just disappear. And he was hoping that if one of the Simons didn't exist—if Mean Simon turned out to not be real in this world—then everything connected to him wouldn't exist, either. If Mean Simon disappeared, then Bunserati would be alive again.

And that was all Danny wanted.

Simon still lay in a heap at Danny's feet, gasping for breath. Danny grabbed him by the shirt and dragged him to his feet. "Come here, Simon," he said through gritted teeth.

Simon continued to wheeze as he stumbled. He managed to laugh quietly. "Okay, tough guy," he said. "Don't hurt me." Then he laughed again and coughed, holding his ribs.

Danny glared at him. "If you fall," he said, his voice as smooth and sharp as a whistling whip, "I swear I'll kick you until you're dead." And he meant it more than he'd meant anything else in his entire life.

Bridget was on the porch. "S-something came over him, I don't know what. He—he just *ran*." She was stammering and out of breath. "I think he's heading into town, Danny. You have to stop him. I'm afraid something terrible will happen."

Danny was afraid of the same thing. But for a moment he stopped and stared at Bridget.

The night had finally made up its mind to assert itself, and as the sky grew darker, the light from the kitchen grew brighter. It was shining behind her—but not just behind her. It was shining *through* her, as if she weren't a girl at all but had become an image superimposed on a photograph, a wisp of something—a hint, like a shadow. She looked as if she wasn't part of the world he stood in, almost as if she existed underneath this world, like an image hovering beneath the surface of a lake.

Danny wanted to tell her to go put on a jacket. It wasn't cold out, but she had her arms wrapped around her and she looked like she was shivering.

But then he heard the screech of car brakes and the sound of metal striking metal. *The bike,* he thought.

He looked at Bridget and she nodded. "Go," she said.

He'd forgotten for a moment that he had the other

Simon by the shirt, but he adjusted his grip and yanked him down the driveway. *You have to choose, you have to choose.* The voice echoed in his head.

"Danny?" his father called from the kitchen window, but Danny didn't stop. He knew the other Simon was at the end of the driveway—knew that the screech and crashing sounds had been his sounds—and he kept dragging his Simon with him, because seeing them both together was his only hope of saving Bunserati.

And if the screeching and the crash were what he thought they were, then this was his only hope of saving Simon, too.

But he wouldn't be able to save them both.

Danny recognized the car immediately, and then he saw his mother standing over the bicycle. She'd hit it square and tossed it almost fifteen feet. The front tire was completely warped and jammed against the fork, and the frame was almost bent in half. The back tire turned slowly around and around, the soft ticking of the gears counting the half seconds. Simon lay a few feet in front of the bike. His body looked as crumpled as the front tire.

Danny's mother heard them scuffling down the driveway, and when they were close enough, she looked at him. "He just . . ." Then she put her face in her hands and cried.

Danny let go of Simon's shirt and started walking slowly toward her. There was blood on the road and Simon's clothes were torn. His legs and arms lay in awkward and unnatural positions, as if he were made only of flesh, with no bones. He looked completely peaceful and in incredible pain at the same time. Their mother just cried and cried.

Danny wanted to cry, too. But the words in his head wouldn't stop. *You get to choose, you get to choose.* He squatted down and tried to think. *Do something*, he thought. *Do something. Choose something.*

One of the reflectors from Simon's bike had broken off and was lying in front of him. It seemed to shimmer in the headlights when he picked it up. He stared at it and tried to make some sense of things, tried to decide if he wanted the reflector to be real or not. *Can someone really choose something like that?* he wondered. What if Bridget was wrong? What if this was all a dream? But the shuffle of feet behind him shook him from his thoughts and made him turn. Simon was stumbling behind him, laughing again.

Danny looked at his mother quickly, but he could tell that she could neither see nor hear the Simon he'd dragged down the driveway. They were parts of different stories, and Danny was the only one who could read them both. But Danny knew what he had to do. This was the moment when he would have to look in the box and see what had really happened, see which "cat" was real.

He stood up, put the reflector in his pocket, and closed his eyes. Deep inside, he didn't want to look. The choices were terrible. Mean Simon belonged to the father in the barn and a dead rabbit. Happy Simon belonged to Bridget. And now Danny had to choose. Either Simon was seriously hurt or Bunserati was dead and Bridget was . . . he couldn't even think it. But if Bridget was right—and he wasn't even sure he *wanted* her to be right, but if she was—looking at them now would tell him which was real. Just like the cat. Just like the waves. Behaving under their own rules.

It was so unbelievable and so incredibly unfair. *What kind of world behaves like this*? he thought. *What kind of world is so random and unpredictable and impossible*? And it *was* impossible. The whole scene was absolutely impossible—except that Bridget insisted that it wasn't, that in the quantum world this kind of thing happened all the time. It was as if they were all living in two different worlds: a world that they knew because it acted the way it should; and then underneath that world, another world that was completely different, that did nothing the way they expected. And somehow their family had stumbled into that world—somehow he'd brought them here. They were living a quantum July, and Danny was so *angry* that this had happened, he could barely stand it.

Simon was right beside him when the hot core of dark rage inside Danny burst for the second time that night. He grabbed Simon by the shirt and pushed him as hard as he could toward the crumpled bicycle. He wanted to push him as far away as he could possibly go, push him out of their life and out of this universe. And that was what he tried to do. He pushed him so hard that they both fell over. It would have been almost comical, except that Danny was screaming, screaming as loudly and as hard as he ever had. He screamed until his breath gave out, and then he gasped and choked and tried to scream some more, as if

the whole problem lay in his lungs and he had to do everything he could to purge it from there.

Finally, exhausted, he stopped.

The memory of his own voice rang in his ears, and he lay in the driveway with his eyes closed, afraid to look. But then he did look. He had to, even though, down deep, he already knew what he would see, knew what, in his heart, he had already chosen.

Simon gathered himself and rose in front of him, that sickening smile on his face. Then he laughed and ran up the driveway.

The lights from his mother's car were gone and Danny was there alone—no accident, no bike, no mother. And the real Simon—the Simon he'd chosen—was running back to the house, laughing.

Which meant that Bunserati was dead. And his mother was gone, probably gone for good. And Bridget?

Danny's head swam and he rolled to his knees to steady himself, to keep from throwing up. When the wave of sickness passed, he was able to sit and open his eyes. And yet something still felt different, changed. He couldn't make sense of it until he reached into his pocket to see if the reflector was there. His pocket was empty. And then it was all clear to him. Just as Bridget had suggested, the two worlds were completely separate, and once the choice had been made, once Danny had chosen Simon the rabbit killer and the dead Simon had disappeared, everything that that Simon had touched, everything connected to him, had also disappeared. And that affected not just the present, but also the past. It wasn't just that the dead Simon no longer existed. He had *never* existed.

It was getting darker, and Danny noticed that his shirt was soaked in sweat and he was starting to get cold and dizzy all over again. Then he stood.

Bunserati was dead—he was sure of it. And no matter what the quantum world might be able to do, it couldn't do anything about that.

But, he said to himself, it could still give him the barn.

18

He would have gone right there if he hadn't noticed something as he passed the house—something so strange he couldn't make sense of it.

The reflector was in his pocket again. Simon's reflector. The dead Simon. The one he hadn't chosen. He pulled it from his pocket and stared at its flickering surface, the dance and play of red and white light. He put it back in his pocket and turned to the house.

He went to see Bridget first, but she was already in his room waiting for him.

"You're here," he said, his voice filled with relief.

She smiled sadly. "Sort of," she said.

"I put them together. The Simons."

"I know," she said. Then she held up her hand and he watched as it flickered and faded in front of him.

He'd chosen the wrong one, he knew that. In wanting to save Simon, he'd lost Bridget even further.

"Wait," he said, suddenly remembering. "Look. I have this." He pulled out the reflector. "This is from Happy Simon—I mean, the Simon who knows you. If I chose the *other* Simon, why is it that I can have this?"

She shook her head. "Let me see that." She turned the reflector over in her hand. "It looks like Simon's. But why? It *should* exist in the other world. What's it doing here?" she asked herself. "Unless . . ."

"Unless what?"

"Unless it's not over, Danny. The only way this makes sense is if you haven't actually chosen yet after all. If you've truly chosen, then the two universes divide and completely separate. But they haven't. Here's one piece of data," she said, holding up the reflector. "And here's another," she said, holding up her hand. "The reflector and I are still here. And that can only mean that there's another choice to make—a bigger choice that you haven't made yet. Or maybe you've already made it."

"Why do you think that?" he asked.

In response, Bridget held her hands up to him again. It looked as if they were only partially there, as if they weren't entirely solid. "It looks like you're still choosing, doesn't it? But you have to admit, if you were to bet on this one, you wouldn't put your money on the disappearing girl, would you?" Then she dropped her hands and sighed. "It's just like with Dad and Jerome. He never actually chose to go to Tibet or to stay with us, but the choice was eventually made for him. The same thing will happen with you, too. The longer this goes on, the more permanent one of these worlds will become. You *can* control it, but your choices have consequences, which is something you haven't ever had to come to terms with. Maybe that's why you never choose. Like Dad, you're afraid of the consequences. But even if you don't choose, a choice will be made, and choices are permanent. And this"—she held up her hands again for emphasis—"this is just a hint of what choices can do."

Danny walked to his desk and stared out the window at the barn. He still had time. He could choose Bridget. It wasn't too late. But then he heard the faint snapping of a whip coming through the window, sounding far away, almost as if it were a dream.

"I can hear it," she said.

He turned, as if the truth had grabbed him by the ear and yanked him around. "Can hear what?"

"The whip."

"Bridget," he whispered. And he wanted to say, "I'm sorry," but the words wouldn't come.

"How?" he finally asked.

"I don't know," she said. "Maybe the worlds are getting closer and closer together. Maybe the quantum world is about to choose for you."

Danny stood at his desk and ran his hands along the back of his chair. There was something he had to tell her. She had to know the truth about what he had to choose between. Someone else had to know, and there was no one else to tell. "There was a year," he said, "maybe two years, when he wasn't home. He was in Tibet."

"Before I was born," she said.

Danny nodded. She knew. She knew it all.

"So we can't both exist, then, can we?" she said. "If you choose the father in the barn, you lose your sister. If you choose your sister, you lose the father you've always dreamed of having. We're from different universes—the result of two very different choices."

He didn't say anything. What could he say? Then he turned to her and almost pleaded. "Can't you do something that will reverse this?" he asked. "Can't you just do a subtraction problem or something that I could carry around to make this all okay?"

She smiled. "It isn't like the commutative property. We're dealing with the quantum world, and the quantum world—"

"Has its own rules," he said, finishing her sentence for her again.

She smiled, but less sadly this time. "It makes me *so* happy that you're paying attention."

"It's getting harder and harder not to."

She nodded and pushed her glasses up. They were the most solid thing about her.

"So what are we supposed to do?" he asked.

"Not 'we,' Danny," she said. "You. What are *you* supposed to do? It wasn't the formulas. You know that. It was you. It was always you. So what are *you* supposed to do? That's the question."

"And the answer is?"

"The answer is, I don't know," she said. "I think you should keep doing what you've been doing. It feels like that's something you're supposed to do."

"But how will I know? What if I'm supposed to do something else and I don't know what it is?"

"You'll know," she said, laying a hand on his arm. "You'll know."

He turned to her then. "I think I know what I have to do."

He spoke with a kind of determination, as if he wanted to reassure her, but she just smiled at him. Then she turned and started to leave.

But at the door she stopped.

"What is it?" he asked.

She sighed. "I haven't told you something, Danny, something very important."

"So tell me," he said, his voice almost frantic.

She smiled. "It's very hard." Then she closed her eyes and raised her head to take a deep breath. When she opened them again, her face looked deliberately composed, as if she was trying to control a deep fear.

"This evening, around dinnertime, I was standing in the hall." She pointed absently to the door. "It was silly, really. I was looking at my feet and my hands. I was having one of those moments when I was, you know, there and not there." She tried to laugh. "Having an undermoment, I guess you'd call it." She reached her hand out to steady herself against the door.

"B? Are you all right?"

She held up a hand to stop him. "Anyway, I was standing there when I heard you coming up the stairs with your pizza."

"I don't remember seeing you in the hall," he said.

"I know."

"What happened, B?" His voice was very quiet.

She took another deep breath. "I remember how hopeful the sound of your feet made me. So much has been changing, you know? But you have always been the same. You've always been, I don't know, solid. Sometimes I'd see you in the underuniverse talking with Simon, but every time you got close to me, you'd blink or shake yourself and you'd see me, right in front of you, you know?" She stopped and lowered her head as if she needed to catch her breath.

"What happened, B?"

"You didn't see me."

"What do you mean?"

"I mean you walked right past me and your arm . . ."

"What about my arm?"

"Danny, you passed right *through* me! Like I wasn't even there. Like I was a ghost!"

19

The barn was dark. There wasn't a light on anywhere and Danny had to feel his way along the center corridor and then up the ladder. He used the sharp snapping sound of the whip to guide him.

As he lifted his leg onto the first rung, he could feel the reflector from Simon's bike dig into his thigh. The dead Simon's bike. The bike that no longer existed.

Or was it the bike that no longer existed in his *other* life?

He stared up through the hole in the darkness toward the sound. He really knew so very little about this life in the barn. He knew his father's stories; he knew his father's dreams. But did he really know his father? Did he really know the past the way he needed to? He needed to know what he was choosing between.

The snapping stopped as soon as his head poked through the floor of the loft. Danny's eyes were still trying to adjust to the dark. But in the corner he saw a shadow

191

shifting in front of the slats, through which the softest hint of moonlight sifted. He raised himself through the trap and felt his way to the bales of hay against the wall. He sat down as quietly as he could and just listened. Even if he'd wanted to talk, he couldn't think of what he would say.

This wasn't his world. This wasn't his life.

Or was it?

"So, I was thinking," his father said from the darkness. His voice was calm and casual, as if they'd been talking for hours.

Danny just waited.

He heard his father clear his throat, and underneath that, the whispering of the whip moving through his hands. "I was thinking that maybe we should just go—you know, pack up, say our good-byes, just leave—and maybe head to, I don't know, St. Petersburg or somewhere. We could join the Russian circus. Think about it. You can use this whip like no one I've ever seen. And I've been working on a new technique I want to teach you. Want to see it?"

"Yeah, sure."

Danny could sense his father smiling at him through the darkness, and a strange feeling came over him. It was pride. He'd never felt it before, not really. And now there it was, soft and almost imperceptible, like a pocket of warm air, and he noticed how comfortable it was, how good it felt just to be in it. He was proud of his father. It was the way he had always wanted to feel. It was the way he wanted to feel all the time.

There was movement in the corner. His father was setting up the cans. One can, though, wouldn't stay where it was placed. Once, twice, three times it tumbled from its perch and rattled to the floor, until his father, in a split second of fury, stomped it flat.

"God! Damn! You!" his father shouted, each word punctuated by a stomp of his foot as he crushed the can into the floorboards.

The anger was so sharp and concentrated that it startled Danny. He heard his father's breath as he mumbled darkly in the night air. He listened as his father searched for, found, and then placed another can on a bale. It balanced perfectly. Then Danny listened as his father took his position somewhere toward the center of the open space.

"Ten cans," he announced. "You hit each can twice. The first hit launches it into the air, the second hit tosses it into a pile near the far beam. At first we'll practice in the day, but eventually you'll do it either blindfolded or in complete darkness." He breathed and let the air out slowly, as if he were getting into character. But for a second he broke the silence and spoke to Danny in an aside. "It's a trick Jerome taught me, years ago," he said. "I could never seem to get it right, but I've been practicing. Ready?"

Danny just nodded. Then he heard it: the soft hissing of the whip in the air, the whistle of speed and power that wasn't power but only the potential for it, the whispered anticipation of the moment when speed became substance. That was the wonder of the whip—that it was motion and speed, and then in an instant it ceased to be an action and became a thing, a point, a hard, sharp, powerful fact that struck a can like a rock and launched it ten feet into the air. It was action and it was fact, movement and thing. And in the whispering moments, it was both things at the same time. It was sound and matter, water and rock, wave and—Danny's breath caught in his throat—wave and particle. It was both.

Was that what Bridget had been trying to explain to him? The properties of a whip? His mind raced back to the lectures she'd given him, the things she'd said. Could the whip be the secret? For a moment the mysteries of the quantum world came together for him, were *almost* clear, when—the *crack-ping* of the whip shook him back into the present.

The first hit, just as his father had predicted, launched the can into the air. That was the *crack-ping*. Danny held his breath and then—*crack!*—the can, as if punched out of the air, went clattering to the floor on the far side of the loft.

He could feel his father smiling.

And then, once he'd established a rhythm, the cracks came more evenly. *Crack-ping, crack, crack-ping, crack, crack-ping, crack*—each can rolling and clattering into the corner. He counted four, five, six cans.

But with the last three cans something happened. The *crack-ping* launched each into the air, but the louder *crack* rang hollow and each can fell to the ground near where it had begun. He'd missed, first once, then again, and then again.

At the third miss, he cracked the whip more loudly than Danny had ever heard before, shouted "Dammit!" with the crack of it, and threw the whip to the floor. He walked toward the three cans and stomped them each four or five times until they were flattened on the floor.

Danny's whole body went rigid. He'd never seen his father like this before. His father's rapid, shallow breathing was all he could hear.

"Well," his father said, laughing weakly as he tried to catch his breath, "guess I need some more practice." He paused. "I let the energy get away from me there. Guess I wanted it too much." He paused again. "That was always my problem, wanting too much." Danny could hear him try to smile. "Got seven, though."

"Yeah," Danny said, trying to sound encouraging and normal, "seven is really good."

"Sure it is," his father said, but his voice was tight. "Come on," he said. "You try it."

"I don't think—"

"Take the whip."

Danny walked slowly to the center of the room. It was very dark, but he could just make out the spot where the darkness was more solid, more concentrated. His father. He nervously reached out and touched the whip.

It felt heavy and warm, but as he let it out, the weight became a kind of energy that flowed through him. His breathing, he noticed, had slowed. He closed his eyes.

He heard his father behind him, stacking the cans. Then he heard him move to the side.

"I can't see them," Danny said.

"Let's just see what you can do. You're a natural at this, Dan. Just try."

"Okay."

Danny kept his eyes closed and breathed deeply. The whip was moving but he didn't feel like he was moving it. The movement of the whip, the energy from his arm—they were one.

And it felt as if he were in a dream, as if the life he was imagining were so real that everything else fell away and he was living it. It made him feel . . . hopeful. It made him feel as if *he* could *make* his own future.

Then the whip struck out—*crack-ping crack, crack-ping crack.* He hit one, two. He wasn't counting the cans initially. He was too wrapped up in the possibilities, the power of hope and potential. But then he began to count—five, six, seven, eight—and the dream faded. He tried desperately to hold on to it, and then he felt his arm tighten. He had just two cans left and he flung out the whip again and again. *Hit them!* he said to himself. *Hit them!*

He missed the last two cans entirely.

The last hollow cracks of the whip faded into the darkness and no one moved. Then he heard his father walk slowly to the bales. He kicked the cans as he went. "You didn't concentrate," he said.

"It was my first time."

"I don't care if it was your *fiftieth* time," his father said. "If you don't concentrate, you'll *never* hit them."

"Sorry," Danny said quietly.

His father sighed. "Don't worry about it. You got eight." Danny could feel him force a smile in the darkness. "That's better than your old man. Maybe we make the trick an eight-can trick. Then we're *perfect.*"

"I guess."

"You hit ten, though, and I'm telling you, the sky's the limit. Big Apple. Ringling Brothers. You can go *anywhere* with a trick like that."

He walked over and took the whip from Danny's hand. "You did good. You really did."

"Thanks."

"Listen, Dan," he said after a moment. "I gotta get out of here." He ran his hand over his head and looked at the ceiling of the barn. "I don't know. I guess I'm feeling a little too cooped up in this barn, if you know what I mean."

"Yeah," Danny said. "I know what you mean."

"So what do you think, you know, about heading out?"

Danny remembered the paper in his pocket and how, when Bridget first handed it to him, it had changed, becoming a flyer with a picture of elephants and writing that was so foreign. "To Russia?"

"Why not? You've got talent, Dan, there's no doubt. You don't have Ringling Brothers talent, not yet, but I'm thinking you could get some good experience and some great exposure in Europe. What do you say?"

"Really?" Danny asked, his ears still ringing with the sound of stomping boots and mangled aluminum. "You really want to go? To Russia?"

"Can you think of a better place? Imagine the things we'll see, the things we'll do."

"What about Canada?"

His father sounded tired. "I think I need to get a bit farther from here, if you know what I mean."

"But what about everyone else?"

His father laughed. "Everyone who? Your mother? There's Simon, of course, and he can come along if he wants." His voice trailed off.

"I don't think Simon likes me very much."

"No. He's a little possessive about the whip, I guess. But he'll come around."

That sounded pretty unlikely to Danny.

"We can't just leave, can we?"

His father laughed. "We're not *abandoning* anyone," he said. "We're following a dream." He paused and Danny felt him move closer. Then he was right beside him.

"Listen, Dan, it's hard to understand, but I need you to try. I've been taking care of you and your brother and, you know, keeping an eye on your mom in a way for years, and the whole time, I've had this feeling that I'd somehow taken a wrong turn somewhere, that my life wasn't really my life at all." He paused. "I don't know if you can under-stand that feeling at all," he mumbled, "but when you feel it, it's one of the worst things in the world."

Danny stood silently, but inside, his whole body felt twisted. It was as if he'd bumped into himself on the street, and he was both shocked and frightened, and yet also in-credibly curious.

"Do you know when it happened? When you lost your way?" he asked.

"In Tibet, I think. But that was a strange time."

"The second time?"

"Yeah."

"But you saved Jerome, didn't you?"

"Yeah, I did."

"So that's good. That had to feel like the right thing."

His father paused. "I thought it would. But he was so mad at us—his sister, Julie, and me. He told us he wished he were dead rather than saved by us. He said hurtful things. Called us selfish and weak. Selfish? After all we'd done for him, all the sacrifices we'd made."

"So what did you do?"

"Julie went home. I . . . well, I didn't have a home, really. Not with your mom. That was something I had to work out later."

"Where did you go?"

"India. Taiwan. Just wandered around. I had the whip and that helped."

"Jerome gave it to you?"

"Yeah, how did you know? Well, he gave it to me once and then told me I couldn't have it. Said I wasn't worthy of it anymore. So I took it and left the monastery. I needed it. For protection if nothing else."

"You *took* it?"

"It wasn't stealing. He *had* given it to me. Don't you see?"

"Sure."

They were silent a moment. Then his father reached out and touched Danny's shoulder. "I want you to come with me, Danny," he said. "Do you want to come?"

"Yeah, of course I do."

"Tomorrow."

"Tomorrow?" Danny asked. "That's soon. Don't you think I need more practice?"

"We'll get you plenty of practice on the boat. Ever been on a tanker ship?"

Danny shook his head. *Tomorrow?*

"You'll love it. That is, if you're sure you want to come."

"Tomorrow?"

"You have a better idea?"

Danny shook his head again. *Tomorrow?*

"Okay, then," his father said, giving Danny's shoulder one long squeeze and then patting him roughly on the back. "It's a plan. But listen"—he'd moved away from Danny and was gathering the cans again—"I want to do this soon. Early morning. At seven-thirty I'm heading out. I've planned it for a while, but I can make room for one or two more if you're really interested. But no pressure. If you're here at seven-thirty, then we'll go together. If not, I'll contact your mother and she can take over. Sound like a plan?"

"Seven-thirty?" Danny said.

"That's right. Now get out of here. I've got some practicing to do."

Danny felt his way to the opening in the floor. But on the second rung, just before his head disappeared, he stopped. "Dad," he asked, "how do you know it's the right dream?"

"What do you mean?"

"I don't know," Danny said quietly. "I have a lot of dreams and I know they can't *all* be the right dream for me. One of them is the right one, but I can't tell which one it is." He stopped and thought of his notebooks and all the

*National Geographic*s he'd studied, all the lives he'd made up for himself. "How do you know which dream is true?"

"Ah, the truth is what you're after, is it?" He could feel his father smiling in the darkness. "Well, let me suggest something to you. There are things you will hear that are true, and there are things that you will make up that are also true. You both receive and create your own truth. Now the question is, what kind of truth will you create?"

Danny stood for a moment.

"I'm creating my truth in Russia," his father said.

"Russia," Danny said, and all his dreams blended together into one dream: the Russian circus. It felt so good, so right. He could live a dream. Why shouldn't he? "See you," he said. Then he was down the ladder and heading out of the barn.

He should have started packing, but he heard something that stopped him.

20

The sound was coming from the far side of the garden, behind the tomato plants, near the pumpkin and squash patch. He turned and walked along the edge, stopping every few steps or so to listen. It was dark, but he could make out the paths in the moonlight.

The garden was huge, almost seventy feet wide and a hundred feet long. His father had drawn a map of the plantings and had every section color-coded, the labels placed at the four primary entrances to each section. Danny turned onto the blue path that led into the corn, but soon turned off the path and followed a more direct route that Simon had cut during his slashing raid. He moved carefully, stepping over broken stalks and rotting vegetables.

The sound got clearer the deeper into the garden Danny moved. Then he recognized it as a voice repeating the word *air*. The voice was mournful, almost as if it were in pain, the words so plaintive and sad: "Air . . . air . . . air . . ." But when he rounded the pumpkin patch, the sound got clearer. And then he knew. It was his father, and he wasn't saying "air," he was saying "Claire."

"Dad?" Danny said.

His father practically jumped out of his skin. "Danny," he cried, leaping to his feet and quickly rubbing his face and head with the back of his hands. "Good Lord, you scared me. What are you doing here?"

Danny didn't know what to say.

A weak smile pulled at his father's mouth. "Well, I'm glad you're here, I suppose." He wiped his eyes again, this time with his sleeve, and sniffed. "It's funny, really," he said, still trying to smile, "but I have no idea where I am."

"You're in the cucumbers," Danny said.

His father looked a little surprised. "So I am. The cucumbers. Not doing too well, are they?"

"Not this year."

"No." He tried to wipe the dirt from his hands and the seat of his pants. He was wearing his SuperValu uniform.

"Dad? Are you okay?"

"Yes. No. I don't know." He sat down in the dirt again and rubbed his head, then absentimindedly picked a cucumber from the ground beside him. He held it up in front of them. "It's ironic, isn't it? Me lost in the cucumber patch?" He looked up at Danny and tried to smile. "I guess once a Cuke, always a Cuke."

Danny didn't return the smile. "How?" he asked. And in that one word were so many questions. How did this happen? How is it possible? How do we save ourselves from this mess? Everything.

"That's a good question," his father said. "But the simple truth is that it's my fault." He looked at his clothes—the green jumpsuit, the name tag. He pulled at the material as if it were something he'd found stuck to him. "Your mother's right, you know. I never dreamed of this. This wasn't what I wanted out of my life."

"What did you want?"

"I don't know. Something. Or maybe nothing. It seems there was a time when this life happened to me and I just let it happen."

"Before Bridget was born?"

He looked at Danny. "Yes."

His father breathed deeply, tossed the cucumber into the dirt, and rubbed his eyes under his glasses. Like Bridget's, they were a little too big for him and often slid down his nose. He adjusted them quickly and then stared off into the tomatoes. "That's exactly when it was. Just after you were born."

Danny sat beside him and his father looked at him and smiled. "You were such a beautiful baby, did you know that? And your brother spoiled you so much. I couldn't take my eyes off you—I can't really explain it. I love all my children, but seeing you did something to me." He paused. "And then I read that letter about Jerome. He was sick. Something had gone wrong. His mystical adventure had turned into a physical crisis, and his parents and his sister were begging me to go there and help him. I know I've told you all this before, but I've been sitting here thinking, and that's the moment I keep coming back to."

He ran his hands over his head, his dirty fingers leaving dark marks. "I go over it again and again, and I don't know what happened. I just couldn't choose. I didn't know which life I wanted. It's so rare to be able to choose a life— or maybe we just think it is. Maybe we choose our life every moment we live it. But I had a single choice that was going to so radically influence my life—a true fork in the road. And I had to take one path. I had to choose. But I didn't. I couldn't." He turned to Danny. "You probably don't know what that's like, do you?"

"I sort of do."

He smiled. "It was terrible. But the worst part . . . the worst part was the way it felt to have to live a life I hadn't actually chosen."

"Couldn't you still have gone to Tibet?"

"Oh, I guess so. But the funny thing was, as soon as I heard that Jerome was dead, I knew that going to him would have been the absolute worst decision. Jerome knew that, too. He knew that the best part of me belonged here with a baby boy in my arms. A person can't abandon himself in order to find himself." He plucked a dry stem from a weed at his feet and drew concentric circles in the dirt. Then he scratched them out quickly and looked up at the barn. "But staying and making things right with your mother wasn't as easy as I thought it would be."

"What happened?"

"Nothing. And everything," he said, tossing the stem

next to the discarded cucumber. "Life happened. Bridget came, your mother built the lab, you all grew up. But the most important part of me—the part that dreamed and hoped and looked to the future—that part of me had sort of gone to sleep, I guess. I got trapped in a locked room and couldn't see that other doors were open." He pulled at his jumpsuit again. "This is what they dress you in when you've let yourself get trapped in a room and can't find a way out."

"But you don't have to wear it."

"I know. There are lots of things I could do. I should open that restaurant." He turned to Danny. "You think I should open it, don't you?"

Danny shrugged. "It sounds pretty neat."

His father looked at the barn, whose roof separated them from the moon. "Yeah. I should do it. I don't know why I don't. Something holds me back. It's like I don't even know who I am anymore. And while I puzzle out who I am, I stay the same."

"Yeah," Danny said. Then he asked, "Do you ever think you might be someone else and this life is all some kind of mistake?"

His father looked at him and smiled. "I feel that way a lot." He rubbed his head again.

Danny looked at the garden, the shadows and the disorder under the silent barn. "But it doesn't *have* to be this way, does it?"

"No, I guess not. But your mother . . ."

Danny waited. He tried not to breathe.

"I think I used up my last chance with your mother. She can't bear the sight of me, to tell you the truth."

"But she loved you once," Danny said.

"Yes," his father said. "She loved me. And that banana bread."

Danny laughed. They could use some magic right now, he thought. Because everything had changed. His father was right. "Can't you whip up a batch?" he asked.

"I think we're long past that," his father said, rubbing his thumb in the dirt and watching it break into dry clumps. "The bread, this uniform, everything reminds her of the person I've become. And it's *that* person that she can't stand the sight of. And the worst part of it all is that I've not only lost the love of my life, I've lost the rest of the story, too."

"Us."

"All of you," he said. "Your mother sat in that family meeting and practically *begged* me to stand up and claim you. And I didn't do anything."

"But can't you change that?"

"I don't know. It would mean being a different person. Can a person just choose to be different?"

"If you can choose to be the same," Danny said, "then why can't you choose to be different?"

His father smiled. "That's a really good point. How did you get so smart?"

"My sister is a genius."

Then they heard someone at the edge of the garden calling Danny's name.

"I'm over here," he shouted, and in a matter of seconds Simon burst through a stand of Indian corn, out of breath and confused. He still looked angry, but less malicious, if that was possible. Something in his eyes had softened, and Danny for the first time understood that what he had thought was anger was really fear.

"Dan, there's a girl." He stopped and looked first at Danny and then at their father. "Dad?"

"Simon?"

"I thought you were leaving," Simon said, his face darkening. "I thought you'd already left."

Simon can see him, Danny thought. He reached into his pocket. The reflector was still there. The reflector from Simon's bike—the *dead* Simon. But if Mean Simon was standing in front of them, and this was his father, and Danny had the reflector, then something very strange was happening.

"No," his father said. "I'm not going anywhere."

Simon nodded. "Good. I wasn't going with you anyway," he said, and his voice was hard, almost a challenge. "Sleeping with rats, eating stale bread and rotting cheese. You can call it an adventure if you want, but I call it homelessness."

"I'm sorry?" his father said, looking first at Danny and then at Simon. "What are we talking about?"

"It's nothing, Dad," Danny said. *They can see each other,* he thought. *It's not too late.* "Simon?" he said, his voice urgent. "What's going on? What girl?"

Simon's face hardened again as he turned to Danny. "There's a girl in the house. I think she's in trouble."

"Bridget?" Danny asked.

"Yeah. Bridget somebody."

"Bridget *Parsons*?" their father said. "Your sister?"

"My what?"

"Never mind," Danny said. "What's happening to her?"

Simon looked at his father and back at Danny, his face a mask of confusion. "I don't know who she is, but she's in trouble, Dan."

"Trouble how?"

"It sounds crazy, but she looks like she's . . . disappearing."

Danny stood quickly. "Where is she?"

"In the guest room—or it *used* to be the guest room."

"The guest room?" their father said. "What guest room? Danny, what's going on?"

"I'll explain later." To Simon, Danny said, "What exactly did she say to you?"

"She said to find you. That it might be too late. That you might not want to help her. She even said I might never find you."

Danny turned and looked toward the barn.

"Why would she say that, Danny?" Their father asked. "What's happening?"

"I'm not sure."

His father rose and stood beside him.

Simon looked at his father more closely. "What are you wearing?"

His father pulled at his jumpsuit. "I'm not sure," he said. Then he turned to Danny. "I don't know if it makes any difference, Danny, but I'm right beside you."

Danny turned from the barn and looked at his father. He was tall, dressed in green, his eyes red-rimmed and large, and he was standing in the cucumber patch. It was almost comical. And when he pushed his glasses up onto his nose, an act so characteristic of the Parsons family, Danny almost laughed out loud. But his father was beside him. He was with him and he wanted to save Bridget. He wanted to save them all. Even if it meant changing himself.

"Okay," Danny said to them, "but I'm not sure I know what to do."

His father put his hand on his shoulder. "We'll figure it out."

21

Danny burst through the door of Bridget's room, but as soon as he was inside, he felt confused. For one thing, the room was completely neat and orderly. In fact, it didn't look like Bridget's room at all. But what really shocked him was seeing Bridget at her desk. He thought at first that she was shaking with cold, her body shivering before him. But as he stared more closely he realized that she wasn't shaking at all. She couldn't be shaking. She was barely there.

He panicked. "B!" he shouted, moving quickly toward her. "B, what's happening?"

She turned from her desk. Her eyes flashed bright and hard as if light were the most definite thing about her. "You came," she said, her voice almost like a whisper of air through a crack in a window.

"B?" he said again, standing beside her desk.

"I'm just reading," she said matter-of-factly.

"But you're sitting down."

"Yes," she said. "It just seemed easier. I've been getting so tired lately."

"But what is it? What's happening?"

She smiled at him sadly. "It can't go on forever, Danny," she said quietly. "The universe is going to choose for itself if you don't." She held up her hands and stared through them. "And it looks like the universe isn't going to choose me."

"No," he said. "There's still time. Quick, give me a formula. Give me something. I can stop this. I can!"

"We've talked about this. It's not up to me anymore. It never was."

"Don't say that," he said, but he knew she was right. It had nothing to do with her.

It had to do with him.

He moved to touch her but stopped himself. His arms shook with fear and indecision. "Don't move," he said. "Don't move and don't disappear. Do you hear me?"

She nodded and almost smiled at his boldness. "I don't know if all this bossiness suits you entirely," she said to him, "but I like it." Then her eyes flashed at him and she tried to stand.

Danny turned to the doorway. His father and Simon stood waiting for instructions.

Then he turned to Bridget. "Simon is here," he said.

"I know," she whispered. "I had to introduce myself."

"He's not our Simon."

She nodded. "I know. But you know that our Simon is dead."

He nodded.

She held up her hand and passed it in front of her face. It moved almost like a shadow, like a heavy veil. At the edges he could see right through it. "I guess," she said, "that for each of us there's a universe where we don't exist." She stared at him hard. "You know that, too, don't you?"

He couldn't look at her.

His father, watching from the doorway, suddenly spoke. "Bridget?" he said. His voice was so soft, so quietly afraid, that Danny thought if a breaking heart could make a noise, it would sound like that. He went to her. "Sweetie, what's happing to you?" His face was a mixture of forced calm and confusion. "Danny?"

"She said you'd know what to do," Simon said from the doorway.

"Danny?" his father repeated. "Do you know what to do?"

Do something. Do something. Danny ran his hand over his forehead. *Think. Think.* He turned to avoid his father's eyes, and then he remembered the reflector. It was still in his pocket.

Suddenly Danny knew. It all made sense. The two worlds had completely overlapped, and Danny was in the middle. The trick was to separate them again so that he was in the world he wanted—the world with Bridget.

But choosing the world with Bridget meant . . . He couldn't think about that now. Bridget needed him.

He thought as quickly as he could. So much had already happened. Each world had itself changed over the past few weeks, as if in the overlapping, nothing was simple and pure anymore. This world had become a part of the other world in certain ways—but not in *every* way. And the question was, how could he save what he needed to save in this world *and* take what they all needed from the other world? How could he save Bridget *and* Simon? How could he save the Cuke *and* the whip? How was it all possible?

And then he had an idea.

"We have to get Mom back."

Simon laughed through his nose. "Oh, good. As long as it's something *easy*." Then his brow darkened. "Give me a break, Dan. What makes you think you'd ever get Mom to come back? She's been gone for a dozen years." He shot a glance at his father, then looked at Danny again. "Would you come back if you'd been abandoned like that?"

"Danny?" his father said. "Why does your brother keep saying the most outrageous things I've ever heard?"

"I'll explain later," Danny said. "Right now, though, I need your help."

"I'm listening," his father said.

"My theory is this." He looked at Bridget; he sounded like a scientist. "What if Mom didn't leave *you* at all, but a possibility of you? What if she didn't really leave Wade Parsons? What if she left, I don't know, the Cuke instead?"

"Aren't they the same person?" his father asked.

"Maybe they are," Danny said, "and maybe they aren't." He paused. "But only you know for sure. Are they the same person?" he asked.

His father stood there brooding for almost a full minute, but nobody laughed or snickered—no one even moved. Finally he turned to his children. "No," he said, his voice strong and firm. "No, they aren't the same person."

"Prove it," Simon said, the flash of fire returning to his eyes for a moment.

"I don't think I can," their father confessed.

"I can help," Danny said. "At least, I think I can. But we have to find Mom. Bridget, do you know where she is?"

"Probably at her apartment, I guess."

"Do you know where it is?"

"Yes. I helped her hang curtains the other day. I can tell you where it is."

"That's not good enough. We have to bring you with us."

"Do you think that's wise, Danny?" his father asked.

Danny nodded. "We have to." He turned toward the door.

"Where are you going?" Simon asked.

"I have to get—" He stopped himself. "You know."

Simon just stared.

"I'll meet you in the van."

He ran as fast as he could to the barn.

22

Inside the barn Danny checked his pocket for the reflector. It was still there, and as long as it was, he knew the two worlds still overlapped. But what he didn't know—what he was hoping for—was that something could be taken from one world and given to the other.

He checked again for the reflector. Still there. Then he reached for the whip from behind the door of one of the stalls, where it was kept. He listened for movement up above, but the barn was silent. He lifted the whip from its peg and held it in his hands as tightly as he could. Then he closed his eyes, counted to three, and leapt through the barn doorway.

He landed off balance and tumbled into the grass. But the whip was still in his hands. He jumped up, gathered the whip loosely in his hands again, and sprinted to the van.

Everyone stared when he climbed in.

"Danny?" his father said.

"I'll explain later," he said, but inside, his heart was bursting with joy. He could see it. His father could see the whip. The most important part had worked. Now he just had to bring the rest of it together. "Let's go," he said. "And we have to hurry."

His father gunned the engine, turned on the lights, put the van in gear, and raced down the driveway. There was a heavy mist in the air and it felt as if it could rain at any moment. Drops of moisture collected on the windshield until they were as big as dimes and rolled down the window. Danny's father ran the wipers every few seconds to clear the window—*chuck-chuck chuck-chuck*. The engine coughed and sputtered slightly. Darkness seemed to wrap the van in a silence, the boundaries of which were defined only by the sounds of the wipers and the engine and Bridget's short, quick breaths.

Their father called from the front, "Where am I going, Bridget?"

"Just past the college," she said, leaning slightly forward in her seat. "Near the Laundromat and that weird used-book store."

"Okay. Hold on."

Simon sat up front with their father. He kept wiping the steam off the windows.

Danny kept his eyes on Bridget, who lay huddled in a blanket beside him in the middle seat. She'd had Simon bring her notebook and a pencil, and she was working on something under the flash of passing streetlights. Danny shook his head every time she looked up at him, but she simply smiled and went back to work.

Then Danny felt her moving beside him, and when he turned, she was sitting up. "I have to tell you something," she said.

"You shouldn't be talking. You need to rest. I'm serious."

She smiled again. She looked as if she'd been trapped somewhere without food or water for days. But Danny marveled at how she also looked happy—almost happier than he'd ever seen her. She practically glowed.

"Really," he said again. "You need to rest."

"Look at me," she said. "Something's happening, Danny, I know, but a nap isn't going to do much to change it."

"I don't care. You shouldn't be talking."

"Just listen. One time. *Please.*" She pretended to whine. "*Please, please, please*, listen to me, Danny." Then she almost laughed, but her body seemed to fade for a moment and she reached out and tried to grab his shirt, as if she needed to hold on to it to keep from slipping away.

Danny felt a wave of panic come over him. "Okay, okay, take it easy," he said. "I'll listen. Just take it easy."

She nodded and held up a finger while she caught her breath.

Their father looked at them through the rearview mirror. "Everybody okay back there?" he asked.

"Yeah," Danny said. "We're fine." Then he said to Bridget, "Want me to tell Dad to take us home?"

"No." That word was the most solid thing about her at that moment. She breathed one more time and smiled.

"Remember," she said, "how in the experiment the cat is both alive *and* dead until someone looks at it?"

"Just like a rabbit," he said.

"Yes." She paused for a moment. "That's actually a good example. Now, think about something for a minute. At that moment when you knew that Bunserati was either alive or dead, what was the one thing you wanted to be able to control?"

"I don't know," he said. "I guess I would have picked which rabbit I wanted to be real—the live one or the dead one."

He could practically hear her smile. "You're so much smarter than you think you are, did you know that?"

"Shut up, little sister," he said.

That made her laugh. "I mean it. You understand the uncertainty principle better than anybody I know. And you get why it's important. You're learning to think like a scientist, to want the same things that scientists want. And what scientists want is the secret to make the uncertainty principle the *certainty* principle. They just want to know how to predict what happens. You wanted to predict it with Bunserati, and scientists want to predict it, too. And they think they can do that by using math formulas."

She started to flicker in front of him, as if she were a lightbulb in a brownout.

"Are you all right?" In his mind he decided that if she did that again, he'd make his father pull over.

She held up her hand again—or what was left of it. The van passed a streetlight and Danny could see right through her hand. She wore a ring that their mother had given her in February for her birthday, and it seemed to hover above her blanket. The hand itself looked more like the memory of a hand than a hand itself. It was as if she were there with them and not with them—and Danny remembered seeing the same thing when he had looked at Simon lying on the road. Before the last time, the time when he had looked to see which was real, he remembered that the reflector from Simon's bike, the one he had in his pocket, had flickered in the same way, as if it were hovering between existing and not existing. Bridget flickered.

"Are you sure you're all right?"

"I'm fine." She was practically gasping.

He looked toward the front of the van again and lifted his hand to touch his father's shoulder. They should turn back.

"No," she said. She reached for his sleeve. "Listen to me. It's coming. It's going to happen soon."

He turned toward her. "What is?"

"The moment." She paused to catch her breath. "The moment when the quantum world can be changed—the moment when you can predict what happens to the cat or to Simon. Or to us."

"How do you know?"

"Look at me!" She held her hands up to his face. "Something is happening here, Danny, and I know you know it is. No one else knows, but you do, don't you? That's why you brought that whip."

He didn't say anything. He didn't nod or even move.

"Yes. I mean, I think so." They were passing the high school; then they'd be at the SuperValu. The college was just beyond that. "Do you know what's happening?"

Bridget shook her head. "Not exactly. Maybe we're about to become parts of a divided universe where you and I, in a split second, suddenly exist in different places and times. Maybe we're traveling in some weird dimension or we're caught in a string of energy that changes us"—she held up her hand again—"that blurs the line between matter and energy so matter *becomes* energy. I don't know." She took a deep breath. "Danny, there's something else about the quantum world you should know."

She looked at Simon, who sat next to their father and stared out the window, his face like a grim, cold stone carving. Without taking her eyes from him, she asked Danny, "Do you think this is the life *he's* always dreamed of?"

"Who, Simon?" He shook his head. "I doubt it."

"I don't," she said. "I think it *is*. I think that's why he's here. He's been given a choice, too. And maybe he's afraid to make it." She looked at Danny. "Do you think he's afraid?"

Danny lowered his eyes. "Yes."

Bridget nodded. "Then he's another person you have to help," she said.

Danny looked at her. "Do you know how?"

She smiled. "There are theories."

He almost laughed and almost cried at the same time. "Tell me."

"There are times—maybe they happen all the time—

when the quantum laws and the laws of the universe finally make sense to each other. At that moment things can be changed, the quantum world can be influenced—I don't really know how. I don't know what you'll have to do, or how it'll happen, or what will be the result. I don't know if you'll be able to influence *us* or *time* or what. But I do know that at that moment, you'll be able to do something to change the way things are one way or another." She pointed to the whip beside him. "Maybe that will help."

He reached over and touched it. "I think it might." Then he smiled. "And do you want to know why? Because it's just like the quantum world. It's both wave and particle. It's water and it's a stone. It moves in waves and it strikes like a bullet. It's both. Just like an electron."

She stretched her hand out to touch him. It was the lightest touch he'd ever experienced, almost like a ladybug landing on his shirt. "I'm glad it's you that is doing this," she said. "I'm glad it's you."

But what Danny really wanted to know was why it was him at all. Why wasn't this happening to Simon? Why wasn't it happening to Bridget?

Bridget read his mind. "It's strange, isn't it? I mean, we can all *feel* that something is happening, and I can understand what's happening, but you're different. I don't know why, but you're the only one who can *see* what's happening, the only one who can go between worlds. I don't know *why* you can or *how* you can, but you can."

"Are you sure this is going to happen?" he said.

She smiled. "I did the math."

Then from the front seat their father pointed off to the right and said, "Is that it?"

"Yes," Bridget whispered.

The street was lined with large Victorian houses that had been converted into offices for lawyers and podiatrists and real estate agencies. Danny read the signs as quickly as he could, but none of the names meant anything to him. Then, as his father slowed the car, he saw what he'd been pointing at. A blue Toyota sedan was parked just half a block ahead of them. It was their mother's car.

"Pull over here," Danny said.

23

She had parked in front of a one-story brick building used as a dentist's office, but on the other side of the street larger brick buildings stood side by side, lining the street. They were the kind of buildings you find on Main Streets in almost every New England town. Shops with large glass windows occupied the lower levels, and the upper stories were used as apartments and offices.

Their father double-parked next to the Toyota.

The block of offices and apartments was on the fringes of the college. There were book and record stores and cafes and bagel shops on almost every corner. The Laundromat and the used-book store that Bridget had mentioned were at the far end of the street. The store directly across from their mother's car was an old drugstore.

Streetlamps cast circles of light on the wet pavement up and down the street. It looked to Danny like the set for a play, each circle of light defining the space where action would take place, a circular stage left near the store, and one stage right near the van. Their father pulled the button for the hazard lights so that the swath of yellow from the streetlights was punctuated by the *tick-tick tick-tick* of orange. *Warning, warning,* it said as it counted the passing seconds.

The rest of the world was silent.

The windows of the old drugstore were decorated with plastic buckets and shovels and Styrofoam floats. A sign in the window said, LIFE'S A BEACH, AND THEN YOU GRADUATE. The college was about sixty miles from the ocean and almost thirty miles from the nearest lake, so it must have been a display for spring break, which had ended about six months ago. The CLOSED sign taped to the window looked like a permanent part of the display.

Without any prompting, their father got out and stood in the middle of the street, facing the drugstore. The hazard lights ticked the seconds, and Danny sat and watched. Then his father lifted his head slightly and called his wife's name.

"Claire!"

The rain had cooled the air, and the apartment windows above the store were open to let in the breeze. Most of the windows were dark, but a few were lit, and the lights cast a warm glow on lacy curtains and venetian blinds. The buildings were still wet from the rain, and they glistened in the street light like the walls of an underground cavern. Their father's voice wasn't really that loud, but there was no mistaking its force. Their mother's name was a fact that he set loose in the night, and it echoed and carried a long way.

"Claire!"

Danny saw a light go on in a third-floor window, and then a curtain rustled. The light wavered a bit as if someone had bumped against a lamp. *That's her,* he thought, and he reached over, took Bridget's hand, and gave it a squeeze. But was he really squeezing her hand? He looked down and thought the night was playing tricks on his eyes. Was her hand there? Then he pulled the blanket back a bit and looked at the rest of her. Yes, it was happening. The rest of Bridget was getting that same transparent quality that had already taken over her legs and hands. The rest of her was disappearing.

"Danny," she whispered.

He put his head down next to her ear. "Don't try to talk," he said. "It's almost over."

"No," she said. She tried to shake her head but couldn't. "No, it's just about to begin. We're getting close. We're getting so close." She breathed. "But remember something. Quantum physics teaches us how conflicting things can still both be true."

"Why are you telling me this?"

"Because you aren't trapped by the surface of things like most people—like I am. You're like Dad in this very important way. Like Dad, you understand things that lie *beneath* the visible world. I bet Jerome understood those things, too." She stopped again. "Do you think it was just a coincidence that Simon brought Officer Stevens to us?"

Danny couldn't look at her or listen to her anymore. First of all, their father seemed to be taking care of things without anybody's help. Maybe she'd been wrong. Maybe this had nothing to do with him after all. Maybe it was their father's actions that were most important. Maybe *he* was the one who was supposed to save them, not Danny.

Their mother had come through a door that led to the upstairs apartments. Her hair was pulled back off her face and she had on a yellow sundress. She walked to the bottom of the stoop and stopped, her arms crossed over her chest, waiting.

"She's beautiful," Danny muttered to himself. And she was. Like in a dream.

"This is it, Danny," Bridget whispered beside him.

Her voice startled him. "This is what?"

"This is the moment. Can't you feel it? Space and time are becoming the same thing. It's all just as the theory says it is." She moved to raise her head again, but he held up his hand. Then she tried to smile, but even that had gone out of her. "Choose well," she said. "Choose well." Danny turned and stared out through the mist and iridescent light. "And remember," she added, "sometimes the best thing a child can do to save a family is to help his parents be the people they're trying to become."

"But I don't know if I *want* to save them. I want to save *you*. And I want to save *Simon*."

"I don't know if you can save us both."

"Then what?"

But Bridget was gone. And so was everything else. Or, almost gone. Bridget and the van seats and Simon behind her, everything was there and not there, gone and not gone. Danny turned to the door of the van but it was gone, too, in a way. The clicking of the hazard lights seemed suspended in a state of half-light, trapped between light and darkness. It was as if the whole world had become a shadow of itself, there and not there at the same time. Everything around him flickered, the way ripples of water play tricks with a reflection.

From far away he heard Bridget call, "Go." And it reminded him of a dream, of a dark-haired girl handing him a piece of paper with bright colors and strange writing and telling him the same thing. "Go." He turned toward Bridget and watched as she tried to push him out of the van, but she couldn't touch him. They weren't really there in the van together anymore. One of them had gone somewhere else, had moved into a different dimension, maybe. He wasn't sure.

Danny stepped out of the space where the van had once been. He could see his father standing in the middle of the street, and he moved toward him slowly, taking each step carefully, as if he were wading through a stream or were a beam of light pushing through a prism. Each footstep felt tenuous, uncertain, as if the ground might disappear on him as well. But he kept moving. And he carried the whip. Of all the things in the van, besides him and his father, it was the only thing that had remained solid, and he took that as a good sign.

"What's happening, Danny?"

"Stay here."

Danny ran to a garbage can that was chained to a streetlight close to where his mother was standing. He lifted the lid and rummaged for cans. There were seven. Close enough. Maybe it was even best.

"Daniel," his mother said. "What's going on? Get out

of that garbage can. Where's your father?" She squinted in the mist. "Oh, there he is. Watching."

Danny ignored her. He gathered the cans and placed them along the curb.

"Daniel," his mother said. "*What* are you *doing*?"

"Mom, please, just stand there. Just watch." He turned and rejoined his father.

"Danny," his father said. "I don't understand."

"I know," Danny said. "I don't either, really. But I think I have to do something right now. See, I've done this trick once in"—he paused—"another place. And I think that if I can do it *here,* with you and Mom, then maybe I can save Simon and Bridget both."

"What do you mean *save both*?" asked his father. "And where did you get that whip?"

"In the barn. It was Jerome's."

"Jerome's? But how did *you* get it?"

"It's a little hard to explain. It's *all* really hard to explain without getting into this whole thing with a dead cat and things that follow their own rules and stuff like that."

"What are you *talking* about?"

"I'm not sure. But will you do this for me? Please? Just stand over there a little and watch."

"Okay, son," his father said. "Do what you think is best."

Danny stood in the street, facing the cans, and breathed. He closed his eyes. He tried to quiet the thumping of his heart and the voice in his head that kept repeating, *You have to do it. You have to do it.* Seven cans. He had to hit them all. Twice. That had to be the answer—the trick to make the two worlds right with each other. To do something in one world that he was supposed to do in the other world—that should be enough to bring the two together.

He hoped.

He felt the whip swing out beside him, felt it move and turn and gather energy. He focused on the sway of his arm, on the rhythm and the quiet whistle it made as it whisked through the air.

Emptier and emptier, his mind behaved like the space outside until it had nearly erased everything except the whip, the cans, and the movement of his arm. There was nothing else. Just those elemental things. It was like a dream.

The sound of the whip hitting the cans made him aware he was even doing it. *Crack-ping crack, crack-ping crack, crack-ping crack.* Effortless and perfect. Until he started counting—and wanting, wanting more than he should, he thought. But how could that be? How can wanting to save people, how can *loving* people be *wanting* too much? Because he did. He wanted them. Bridget *and* Simon. His father the Cuke *and* his father with the whip. He had to save them all. *He had to.*

He felt his whole body stiffen with resolve.

Crack, crack, crack.

The last three strikes of the whip rang hollow in the air. When he opened his eyes and saw the three cans standing on the curb where he'd set them, he knew he'd missed. He'd failed. Three cans. There was a good chance he'd lost them all—Bridget, Simon, his father—everyone.

"That was amazing," his father whispered beside him. "Really, Danny, that was absolutely *incredible*."

230

"I didn't do it."

"Didn't do *what*? Hit them all? Who cares? You got so *close*. It really was something to watch. I had no idea you could do such a thing."

Danny turned to him. The world around them continued to flicker in that uncertain, undefined way, as if they existed in a combination of mist and matter. Nothing had changed. He looked where the van should have been, but it was still lost in a haze, as if the atoms that would arrange themselves into the van, the street, the buildings, had paused midway through the assembly.

Nothing had changed. He'd failed, but maybe it hadn't mattered. Or maybe he'd done the wrong thing. Or maybe it wasn't supposed to be him at all. Maybe it was supposed to be his father who did something.

He turned to his father. "You should expect more of people," he said.

His father smiled. "I guess that's true."

"You should expect more of yourself, too." Danny held the whip out to him.

"That's definitely true." His father looked at he whip. "For me?"

"It is *your* whip," Danny said, and his father smiled and nodded.

He was silent for a moment. "You think I need to do this?" he asked.

"Yeah. I think so."

"Why?"

Danny stared at him. "Remember when you said to me that you felt like you didn't turn out to be the person you wanted to be? You said you let your life happen to you. That's where all this mess came from."

His father nodded. "That's right."

"Well," Danny said, "maybe this is your chance to change that."

"But why, Danny? What is hitting some cans—if I can even do it, which I doubt very much—going to change?"

Danny stood silent for a moment without answering. "I don't know," he said. "Maybe it's a way of finding order in the chaos. Things are pretty chaotic right now. Maybe if you do this, something will fall into place. Maybe something will make sense."

"You sound like Jerome. But what if it doesn't?"

"I don't know. I don't know a lot, really. But I do know one thing: I know what it feels like to not be the person you're supposed to be. I feel that way all the time, and so do you. But now I think I know who I'm supposed to be."

"And?" his father asked.

"I think I'm supposed to be the boy who stands next to you when you use that whip."

His father shook his head. "I don't know, Danny. None of this makes any sense to me."

"Me either. But it makes sense to Bridget. And I think it would have made sense to Jerome." Danny's father stood motionless. The whip hung from his hand, nearly dead. "Please," Danny said. "I think we have to trust him on this one. I think we have to trust ourselves. We have to try. Please," he said again.

His father nodded slowly and then lifted the whip, as if he were measuring its weight and length. "Okay," he said. "I'll try." Then he turned to Danny and stared at him hard. "For us both."

Danny took several steps back and watched. He wasn't sure what was going to happen, he wasn't sure what it would mean, but he knew, inside, that something about this made sense. He didn't know why, but he trusted it. And he'd never trusted anything like this before.

"I haven't done this in a while, you know."

"But you've done it before?"

"A long time ago. It was a trick Jerome loved. How did you say you learned it?"

"I guess the idea came to me in a dream."

"A dream, huh?" His father shook his head and measured the weight of the whip again. "Any tips for your old man?"

"You can't think about it too much," Danny said. "You sort of, you know, find the zone and go with it."

His father nodded. "Like making banana bread."

"Yeah, it's probably a lot like that."

His father smiled and, turning from Danny, closed his eyes for a moment and balanced the whip in his hand. Then he slowly shook the whip back and forth so that its whole length stretched out in front of him. "You know," he said, almost to himself, "I sometimes think Jerome wanted me to have this whip as a kind of lesson."

"Like a metaphor?" Danny asked.

His father nodded. "Yeah, like a metaphor. He was

always talking about how we live our lives with opposites, with things that can't exist together but do. I think he sent this whip to me to make sense of the chaos—of the paradox of living in harmony with incompatible opposites." He stared at the whip and was silent. "I guess," he said, "Jerome knew I'd need it one day."

Danny watched as his father lowered his head and stared at the whip as if he were waiting for it to speak to him, as if it held some deep answer. And maybe it did. Maybe that was the strangest thing of all, that they were waiting for the whip to tell them about this man, to tell them things they couldn't know by themselves.

"Did you ever think," his father said finally, "that the whip is an awful lot like water?"

Danny nodded, but then he realized that his father wasn't looking at him, wasn't talking to him.

"It's so smooth," his father continued. "The way it moves when you swing it or the way it falls to the floor in a shape that's as much a puddle as it is a line. Just like water, really. And when you snap it against something, it's like water then, too, when it crashes against the shore in a storm. Or would you say it was more like a bullet?" he asked, turning to Danny and smiling.

"Like a rock."

His father's smile broadened at his answer, and it was as if the lights around them suddenly brightened.

And then Wade Parsons closed his eyes and began to move.

In the doorway, Danny's mother suddenly came into

clear focus, as if she'd swum to the surface of a deep, clear pool. She stood with her arms crossed, but Danny noticed that she watched her husband as intently as he did.

There were things about his father standing in the street with a whip that reminded Danny of his other father in the barn, his father from another time. But this man in front of him wasn't the same person. He was smoother. His father in the barn had a thoughtless, fluid way with the whip, but this father, the father who hadn't held a whip in years, was using it as if it were something else—as if it were a part of his body, a part of his mind, a part of his spirit. He didn't use it as if it were a source of power to be wielded.

He used it as if it were the truth.

The whip gathered more and more speed in his father's hand. Danny could hear it hum through the air, could almost *see* the sound as it whistled back and forth in front of them all. And then, with a movement that wasn't really a movement, with an action that was more a suggestion or a wish, his father focused the whip toward the bench, and *crack-ping crack!*

Danny realized that his eyes had been closed, and he quickly opened them to see the can fly through the air and land at his mother's feet. His father had done it. He'd hit a can. He'd launched it off the curb and then struck it out of the air. It was the trick Danny had seen his father perform in the barn. The same trick. And he'd done it. Once, anyway. But he'd done it.

He wanted to shout something, to cheer, but then he saw that his father's face was still; his eyes, amazingly, were closed. The whip continued to move in his hand. It wasn't over. It was just beginning. And there were two cans left.

Danny closed his eyes again and listened. And counted.

Again, there was the sharp *crack-ping* as another can was launched into the air, and then the *crack!*—a sound so sharp and loud that Danny jumped. There was power in the way his father was wielding the whip, a power Danny had never imagined his father possessed.

One more, Danny thought. *Just one.* Danny squeezed his eyes closed and tried to will the last can into the air. *Hit it. Hit it.*

Then he heard it. The *crack-ping.* Can number three—the *last* can—launched into the air. Danny could almost see it in his mind as it tumbled through the air, and he waited for the final *crack,* the last sound that would complete the trick and, he was sure, make everything right.

Crack.

Danny never heard a whip sound so empty. The can landed next to where he'd placed it and rolled into the gutter.

His father had missed.

Danny opened his eyes slowly, wary of the fury he was sure he'd see—his father storming to an aluminum can and smashing it with his boot.

But his father hadn't moved. He was standing in the same place, the whip beside him, and he was laughing. He was laughing.

He turned to Danny. "I guess I wanted it too much, you know?"

And then Danny knew exactly what he needed to do—knew who he needed to be. Bridget had been right from the beginning. It wasn't the *doing,* it was the *choosing* that made a difference. And he was supposed to be the boy who stood beside *this* father. He was meant to be that boy.

Danny smiled for what seemed like the first time in weeks. "I choose you," he said out loud. "I choose you."

His father laughed again. "What are you talking about?"

"I choose you," Danny said again.

His father grabbed him around the head and rubbed his hair with his free hand. "Who says you get a choice?" he said.

Danny just looked up at him and smiled.

Then his father turned to Danny's mother.

She had her face screwed up in a pucker and her arms were still crossed.

"Come home, Claire," he said. "Please come home. I know I never said it when it mattered most, but I'm saying it now. I need you. *We* need you." He looked at Danny and smiled. "We seem to be in a choosing mood tonight, so let me add to it. I *choose you.* It's the choice I should have been making all along."

"A lot has happened, Wade."

"I know."

"And it doesn't all go away just because you can use a whip," she said.

"No," he said. "You're right."

"Then why do you think I'll ever come home?"

"I think you'll come home when you see that I'm different—or when you see that I've become again the man you first fell in love with."

She looked at him skeptically. "This better not have anything to do with banana bread."

Danny and his father laughed, and Danny noticed that his mother smiled in spite of herself.

"No banana bread, I promise."

She tightened her arms across her chest. "What, then? What's changed?"

"In a funny way," he said, squeezing Danny around the shoulders, "I've been found."

She made no move off the step, and her face was unchanged for a long while. But as she stood there, the rest of the world came slowly back into focus. Atoms arranged themselves into the shape of a building, a car, a van, a brother, and a sister. Danny heard the soft ticking of the hazard lights, the *chuck*ing of the windshield wipers, and before too long Simon came out of the van looking a little less confused, a little less angry. By the time he reached them, Danny would have said he was almost happy. They both looked at their mother and waited.

And then Bridget came out, too. Still weak, still a little wispy around the edges, but there. And her mother smiled when she saw her.

24

Bridget knocked quietly against the door to Danny's room.

From inside, Danny tried to call to her, but his mouth was full of tacks and pushpins. He grunted through his teeth as loudly as he could and she came in.

"What are you doing?" she asked.

He just nodded to the walls. Small holes marked them in random, almost starlike patterns. Nothing else was there except the slightly discolored sheen of the walls that had been exposed for the past year.

"You're taking it all down?" she asked.

He nodded again, pulling the last pin from the wall and watching a picture of a mountaineer hanging from a long green rope slowly drop to the floor.

"Why?"

"I don't know," he said after spitting the mouthful of pins into his hand. "It just felt dumb, I guess. All these pictures and maps and magazines—they don't really make sense anymore."

"You threw out the magazines?"

"All but the ones with naked Africans. Simon wanted those."

"He's sick," she said, but they both smiled. "But better."

"Almost normal," Danny added.

Danny transferred the pile of tacks in his hand to a small bag he'd set on an empty bookshelf. "Dad home yet?" he asked.

She shook her head. "Mom's meeting him in town for dinner."

They gave each other a knowing look.

"Want to hear the weirdest part? He brought a change of clothes."

"Are you kidding?"

"No, I'm serious. It took him twenty minutes to find a pair of pants that weren't ruined by gardening."

"Is this, like, a date?" he asked.

"I think so."

"Weird."

They stood there, frozen, until a shudder came over Danny and he laughed. "It's like they're kids again."

"I think it's sweet," Bridget said.

Danny rolled his eyes and, grabbing the last few tacks from the window casing, climbed down from his desk chair. "How are you feeling?" he asked.

"Better. Almost good as new." She paused. "Happy, even."

"Happy," Danny repeated, letting the word float between them and fill the spaces.

And it was exactly how he felt. The future seemed to

be set, and, maybe for the first time, set in the ways it ought to be.

Bridget sat at his desk and looked at the only two pictures he'd stuck on his bulletin board. One of them was the photo of their father and Jerome from the living room. The other was the class photo of Sarah Evans. "What are these for?" she asked.

He smiled. "One of them is, I don't know, a piece of history—and a reminder of what was and what might have been, I guess. It makes me feel like things are the way they're supposed to be."

"And this other one?" She pulled Sarah Evans's picture from its thumbtack and read the back. " 'Danny,' " she read, " 'why are you so good at math when you never pay attention? Love, Sarah.' " She laughed. "She thinks you're good at math?"

"Compared to some people, I am."

On the bulletin board there was also a flyer for Smithsonian Travel Adventures. He'd circled a train expedition through India. And on the desk was a book he'd gotten from the library on the Hindu gods. "What's this all about?" she asked.

He shrugged. "The future, I guess."

She smiled. "This future, or another one?"

"This one." He put a few more things into the box on his bed. "It's weird. I've never really thought about *this* future before. I've never found myself just waiting for the good part to happen."

Bridget raised her eyebrows at him. "Do you know what's going to happen, Danny?" she asked.

He made one last adjustment to the pictures, his note-books, and his atlases in the large cardboard box. Then he folded the flaps of the box over each other and tugged at one of the corners until it locked the others into place. "Not really," he said. "I mean, it's not like I know the future. I suppose it's that I finally understand the past." He picked up the box and turned to her. "I'm going to take these to the barn."

Bridget nodded, but then, just as Danny reached the door, she said, "It's all changed, isn't it?"

"I don't know," he said, stopping and turning to her. "You're the genius." He paused, then added, "But it feels weird."

"What does?"

"Everything. You. Me. Simon. Dad and Mom. Even this room. The barn. The picture of Dad and Jerome. Even that picture of Sarah. It all feels like it's changed. And it feels like it's exactly how it used to be, all at the same time."

"And nobody talks about it," she said.

"What could we say? How do you explain it?"

She shrugged.

"Do you really think something quantum happened to us?" he asked.

Clearly, he thought, something had occurred, something deep and profound, but Bridget seemed as confused by it as he was. "It's a little embarrassing," she said, "but I don't actually understand that much about what happened. In fact"—she smiled—"I don't really know much of anything."

But Danny didn't really care what the answer was. The

reasons weren't important to him. "Then you'll have something to learn at the academy."

"I guess. Although I doubt Professor Evans could make any sense of this, either."

He shifted the box in his arms one more time, looked quickly at the photo of his dad, the photo of Sarah, and then he smiled at Bridget.

"I'm just going to get rid of these," he said. "I'll be right back."

    ⚘   ⚘   ⚘

The air in the barn was still and much cooler than in the yard, and Danny breathed it in as if it were the first breath he'd taken in hours. The smell stirred things in him that were vague and painful and strangely comforting. He smiled without knowing he was smiling as he walked in the near darkness to the back of the barn.

As he passed the hook where the whip had been kept, he noticed that it wasn't there, but he found it hanging from a hook beside the last stall, deep in the barn. His father had oiled it recently and it hung there, sleek and almost glistening. Danny put his box in the stall, tucking it behind an old over-turned wheelbarrow. He gathered some rakes and shovels that leaned against the far wall and arranged them beside the wheelbarrow instead, so that they camouflaged the box a bit more.

Stepping back he paused and stood staring at it for a moment. He felt like he'd been saying good-bye to things a lot lately, and now he felt as if he were doing it again. He almost said it out loud. Good-bye. Then he turned and closed the door behind him, latching it carefully.

And there was the whip again. He felt suddenly overcome by a feeling that was completely the opposite. "Hello," he said, this time out loud so that the whole barn could hear him. "Hello," he said again, this time more loudly. And then he laughed. *Let the whole world hear me,* he thought. He was Danny Parsons. This was his father's whip. He had gone back to the beginning of something. He was home.

ACKNOWLEDGMENTS

I am not a scientist and am therefore deeply indebted to physicists who could make quantum theory comprehensible to me. Fritjof Capra's *The Tao of Physics* was a very important book for developing the ideas in *The Quantum July,* especially to the extent that the book explores the similarities between the quantum universe and Eastern philosophy. I am indebted to David Deutsch and his "many-universes interpretation" of quantum physics, and to John Gribbin's book *In Search of Schrödinger's Cat*, which acted as a sort of primer in my journey through this absolutely incredible view of reality.

Thanks also to Glenn Woods for his early interest and sustained enthusiasm, and especially to Erin Murphy and Stephanie Lane, for believing in this book even when its only virtue was its potential. I couldn't have done this without your help.

ABOUT THE AUTHOR

Ron King lives with his wife and their three sons in a small town on the coast of New Hampshire. He is a teacher in the winter and spends his summers throwing batting practice, developing his technique for grilling the perfect hot dog, and writing last year's Christmas letter. This is his first novel.